I0738566

THE NEW REPUBLIC OF TEXAS

E. MANDERVELLT

This is a work of fiction. Names, characters, places, and incidents are either the product of the author's imagination or are used fictitiously, and any resemblance to actual persons, living or dead, business establishments, events, or locales is entirely coincidental.

THE NEW REPUBLIC OF TEXAS

All rights reserved.
Copyright © 2020 by E. Mandervellt.
This book or parts thereof may not be reproduced in any form without permission except for the use of brief quotations in a book review.

FIRST EDITION

ISBN: 978-0-578-83293-7
AIN: 0004538-5612283-5605419

newrepublicoftexasbook.com

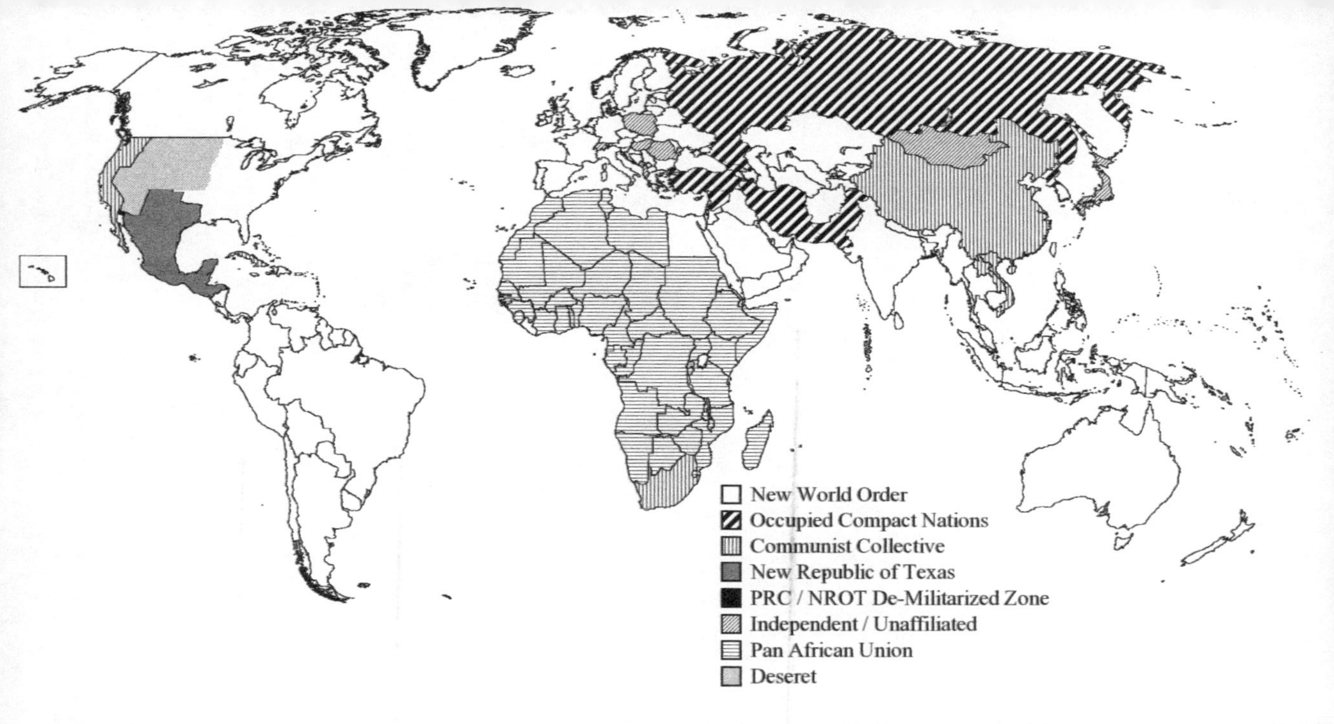

New World Order
Occupied Compact Nations
Communist Collective
New Republic of Texas
PRC / NROT De-Militarized Zone
Independent / Unaffiliated
Pan African Union
Deseret

For Galen

CHAPTER ONE

A lone Guard trudged along the highland overlooking Deseret, stiffly avoiding boulders and shrubs. Sand kicked up by its graceless steps would sometimes sharply pop as it struck the charged air surrounding its heat fins, breaking up the monotonous stomping. For miles around there was no other sound. The Northern Border had seen frequent bombardment and serious conflict since the inception of the Republic and now the area was bereft of wildlife. The rustling of the horned toad, the flight of frightened wrens, the braying of wild asses, none of these sounds were now heard here. Even the flora had been routed leaving only the hardiest lifeforms, often succulents, whose wind-song was softer than the sound of the wind itself. Ecologists and nature enthusiasts had been attempting to restore area wildlife, bringing specimens from the southern Prefectures of the Republic here to the north, but their efforts appeared to have been in vain. It seemed that all the transplanted creatures chose to migrate south and flooded the Dallas suburbs with hundreds of lizards, snakes and desert beetles. Tango Alpha did not know why and was not concerned. He did, however, express amusement at the spike in ladies boot sales shortly after that first expedition, long ago.

On the front panel of the Guard's torso was painted in thick black lettering the call-sign NROT 27 above a lone, five-pointed star. The insignia was well worn and slightly obscured by a patina of chalk and dust swept up by border winds over a decade of service. Large metal fins protruding from the power supply on the dorsal panel were slightly candescent and caused the surrounding air to warp the golden morning light, obscuring the profile of the vaguely man-shaped device. Plutonium, salted with a mixture of cobalt, arsenic, and tin, would power unit Twenty-seven for a further century, if it survived.

The Guard was an avatar for Tango Alpha, the Alderman and Chief Judge of the Republic. Many of these machines, in a variety of designs, were stationed along the border and within cities and townships where they stood watch over the populace from sentinel towers or as they hovered or flew gleaming through the great, Texas sky.

The Northern Border was constantly under siege, either by sorties run out of forward bases of the People's Republic of California, pathetic raids by the tribes of Deseret, or by the steady trickle of emigrants seeking political asylum or a new life within the New Republic of Texas. The United States took a less aggressive stance, preferring to cajole Texas with sanctions and diplomacy into abandoning their independence and rejoining the Union.

This particular Guard regularly served as Chief of Northern Border Control, which entailed dedicated review of satellite and surveillance imagery and the coordination of other Guards and semi-autonomous drones patrolling several hundred miles of the hard, invisible line that separated the order of the Republic from the chaos beyond. Though any Guard could fulfil the role, this unit was the first to manifest it and was left there out of a pride in tradition often demonstrated by the Alderman.

Though recognized by Citizens, Tango Alpha's personality and personhood were little understood. Via executive fiat, Tango Alpha had banned all investigation into his current source code without express permission. Arguing that, having achieved intellect, he was now functionally a person and thus afforded protections against psychologically invasive interrogation techniques as defined in the new Constitution, poring through his mind without consent would constitute torture. Access to server hardware and avatars such as the Guards and other drones was similarly limited, although a team of elite engineers were employed in a constant tech advancement program headed by Tango Alpha himself. These actions did little to quell the suspicions of many, but this could not be helped. Texans were by nature a breed of skeptics. Most conceded that the Alderman offered excellent defense and administration, and any Citizen could speak with him at any time, a gesture much appreciated by a people who took great stock in the idea of looking a man in the eye.

No avatar of the Alderman had eyes, per se. Most Guards had a complex camera centered and three-quarters from the base of the head module. Twenty-seven was one of these units. That camera now scanned the horizon, keyed to the east where an airborne drone had detected unexpected radio transmissions. In all available spectra there was no real sign of a source, yet the transmissions continued, the object moving rapidly on a course that would reach the border within minutes. As the inheritor of Silicon Valley, the PRC had been able to quickly create a very effective Military R&D Department after the war via purchase, trade, and talent. Rumors of their employing new stealth technology had been circling and this appeared to be the first field deployment.

For a moment, Twenty-seven's movement ceased mid-stride. A small shudder ran through its shoulders and it began to walk again. This time, however, its movements were more fluid and its demeanor almost human. The already burdened power supply desperately ejecting heat into the saturated air now glowed outright as it ramped up output to facilitate a fuller presence of Tango Alpha. Border Guards were ancient in comparison to newer avatars and could operate at full capacity for only one half-hour. Damage would occur thereafter.

Have to be quick, Alpha thought. *Let's begin.*

Miles above in the cold silence of space, an orbital weapons platform made a few small adjustments to its geosynchronous position using brilliant purple ion jet-streams. These bursts of light were visible from the surface on a clear day and served not only as fair warning but to intimidate foes of the Republic. Two small, tungsten cylinders emerged from twin drums on the underside of the platform. Each 25 kg payload was grabbed by a robotic arm which positioned the Hammers for a precision strike. Spinning at nearly 2000 rpm, the end effectuators shot down toward the surface and released their payloads before their arms folded up and back into protective shells.

Two other Guards were summoned off their patrols and were now en route to Twenty-seven. Tango Alpha leapt off the ridge and started sprinting toward the designated impact site. The large metal heat fins glowing made a molten streak through the dusty air in the wake of the racing Guard. As Alpha closed the gap, the rough size and speed of the enemy caravan became apparent, and that speed was increasing. This had been accounted for. They had clearly detected the Hammer launch and were accelerating to escape the impact, causing strain on their stealth systems. Infrared trails began to appear behind the group.

Now the profiles of fifteen heavily armored and fully outfitted Abrams X tanks emerged like spectres, warping the heat waves against the backdrop of desert plateaus. Count and identification were confirmed by satellite. These vehicles were dangerous. Tango Alpha focused on the communication feed to Central.

Calmly and with a voice almost that of a rural Texan male, Alpha said, "I have to maintain distance. Going airborne. Get coordinates to Artillery and wait for my signal. Cobalt, 120 mm, impact detonation. Ensure Sol is ready. Copy?"

Twenty-seven halted forward motion with an awkward slide. Jets emerged from each boot and lit, rocketing the Guard hundreds of feet in the air within seconds. Shields emerged from the torso and clasped the heated fins, creating a channeled, radioactive discharge to aid in maintaining attitude. Yet another reason that the lizards always headed south.

"Copy. Alpha, would it not be wise to attempt at least one

capture? I am very impressed with this masking ability. I mean... optical, IR, and UV? That's nuts! Over," offered General John Elliss, technical advisor on watch.

"Irrelevant. These commies ruined my morning walk. Over."

The General chuckled. "Kek. Wilco."

"Thank you, Elliss. Have your men located who they're talking to yet? Delay response for impact. Over." Some tasks were left to humans in the NROT to foster their skills and a sense of self-worth.

Twenty-seven jetted into a decent pursuit vector as Guards Twenty-five and Thirty-nine arrived in the area. Now appeared the Hammers. Camera refresh rates were enhanced so Alpha could better analyse the impact. From three viewpoints and for one long second, he watched as two gleaming, rifled hunks of half-molten metal split the summer clouds and slammed at Mach twenty into the tail end of the enemy cavalry, atomizing one Abrams X and flipping another pair of them out of the fight. A shell of red hot shrapnel bloomed into the regiment, knocking out all the stealth tech and revealing the desert camo death engines emblazoned with the familiar, red and gold banner of the PRC.

A good start, thought Tango Alpha.

Were he human, he'd have been smiling.

CHAPTER TWO

"Three units down!" cried a brown-clad Tank Commander to Fleet Admiral Fowl. His workstation, littered in data feeds of the action happening at the Northern Border, sat above a series of terminals occupied by over a dozen young Pilots, similarly dressed, each in control of one of the fearsome tanks now making a push for their target. Headsets linked to onboard cameras gave them a ground view and a complex interface before each allowed the Pilots to control every aspect of Abrams X operation. No living crew meant the tanks could carry more ordinance and allowed room for a repair drone that could fix minor damage and issues between engagements. Recent defense integration with the People's Republic of China had been fruitful indeed.

"Tango's getting quicker," he continued, as Admiral Fowl walked from her command seat to his desk. "We expected to be discovered but not this soon and We most def didn't expect it to drop Hammers right away. At this rate, We're totally fucked!"

"Maintain, Commander Garret!" Fowl demanded, taking a moment to calm her manner before going on. "Maintain the attack. We cannot afford to waste these Axes so make sure You get to that tower. Failure is not an option. SigInt is moving on the satellite. Our task will get easier once We've disabled it. Pay attention, and watch out for enemy defenses. Also, language?"

Having properly motivated her subordinate, Fowl spun on heel and returned to her chair. Her stride was graceful, confident. The standard fatigues she wore were a compliment to her figure and there was little doubt among the ranks that she was one of the most beautiful women in the People's Army. Despite her nervous outburst, her trust in Commander Garret was strong. Even stronger was her hope that he was free later, as she and her partner were having a spat.

Fowl was a true believer in the Century of Harmony, the social program adopted by the PRC after California, Washington, and Oregon seceded from the Union to form the new State. Its mission was simple: to expunge evil from the human heart by any means necessary. Sadness, failure, pain, even bigotry and phobias were symptoms of a Capitalist system than encouraged trampling on other people to get to the top. The only cure for the Soul-sickness of the age was a benevolent implementation of Gender and Race Communism that would ensure the welfare of the people while allowing them to pursue their truest goals without the constant, poisonous drip of insult, dissatisfaction, and apathy from leadership.

For Fowl, the People's Republic was virtually paradise on Earth. No Comrade went without a meal. Anyone unable to find work on their own was found a healthy and productive task at a plant, farm, or remotely from their home. One could walk down any street in the PRC and never hear so much as an insult and see only smiles. People were allowed to be themselves without fearing a backlash from others while fighting together to create a healthy, happier world.

The new nation was spared most of the failures of other People's Republics due to a number of fortuitous initial conditions surrounding its founding: the presence of Silicon Valley, which made easier the performance of psyops and information warfare; a largely ideologically homogeneous population, which made the adoption of the Science and Century of Harmony less painful; fertile valleys and forests, which fed and housed the populace; and its location on the West Coast, which connected the PRC to her sibling states in Asia. Those who disagreed with Harmony mostly emigrated to Texas or the United States, and far greater numbers immigrated to join the People's Republic post-war.

There were those who continued to struggle against the Century of Harmony, but they were only ignorant to its true meaning. Their misaligned Souls were unable to integrate properly into a truly healthy Collective. Most disillusioned Comrades who survived Therapy went on to lead happy lives, and those that didn't weren't fit for living. Furthermore, based on the Laws of Harmony, their Souls would, upon death, merge with the Universal Vibration and persist until the end of time within the bliss of the All That Is Possible. Thus Humanity, itself like an organism that could be harmed by infection, was scrubbed clean inside the PRC, with the irritants converted to positive Energy. Fowl embraced the Collective's hope that its Truth would free poorer Souls of the world from their selfish and ultimately meaningless ways.

The very existence of the New Republic of Texas, governed by Tango Alpha, which wasn't even human, was an affront to Harmony and even Humanity as a whole. It did them no favors that their Counter Intelligence Division constantly attacked PRC servers to deluge social media with their bigoted propaganda, spamming users with forbidden words and stupid, outdated quotes from Union and New Republic founders. Military actions taken by the NROT were purely defensive, but in the age of information warfare such activity could only be interpreted as an attack. Their absolutist, individualist ideology was a major obstacle for the growth of the Collective and, with their failure to embrace Harmony, they were a major source of Dissonance whose presence could not be allowed to persist unchallenged.

Today's mission was not only a crucial test of the new Stealthy! module, which had far outstripped expectations, but also a critical attempt to destroy up to fifty percent of Tango Alpha's consciousness by eliminating the northernmost server tower housing mainframes used by the AI to be. It would also serve a heavy blow to stubborn Texan pride to destroy the facility where Tango was created and from which it took its name, the Tango Alpha General Intelligence Laboratory, located near the northern edge of the panhandle.

The situation had looked promising. Never before had PRC forces gotten this close to the facility. Despite Commander Garret's negative attitude, the Aura in the room was still good. Each of the Pilots knew they were on the cusp of an historic victory for Harmony and their comfort, engagement, and happiness metrics read accordingly. From her seat, Fowl could monitor conscript brain wave and chemical levels, and every so often she'd give one of the Pilots a little dopamine hit via various available drugs when she noticed a metric like enthusiasm below tolerance.

She did this now to console the young woman who wept quietly for her tank which had been Hammered from orbit. Fowl also sent her a simple message consisting of three small images: tank, fire, facepalm. Cassandra, the weeping Pilot, immediately looked up from her terminal with an adoring smile and a glint in her sodden eyes. She mouthed the words *Thank you, Admiral*, to which Fowl silently replied, *It's O.K. I love You*. The Pilot made a little happy dance as she turned back to her workstation, ready to command one of the incoming support drones.

Those NROT scum don't appreciate the power of positive psychology, Fowl thought. "Get Her into the first Flutter in range, Commander."

"Yes, Admiral. We asked Air to send three but We're going to need more. Are You even watching this feed? Where is SigInt? Look at this shit!"

She noticed an icon on her display indicating a response from Intelligence. It was not good news. "They encountered a problem while attacking the satellite. Seems it's been updated and We are unable to disable it. Prepare immediately for an attack by Sol, Commander," Fowl ordered before giving Garrett the smallest dose of amphetamine.

"Yes, Admiral. Pilots! Assume formation delta and increase speed. In t-minus fifteen seconds switch to zeta patterns and follow the paths You are assigned. Cassandra, You're wing leader for Mark and Princess. Go after those Guards. They'll act as spotters here in a sec."

On the screen before her, Fowl watched the elegant chaos wrought by these orders play out. The twelve remaining Axes spread out from a phalanx into a roughly scattered grid, driving up voluminous clouds of dust as they sped full throttle to the facility. Gauges in the top-left corner showed the distance from Tango. One hundred and twenty-five miles. Range on the tank cannons was roughly fifteen miles. They still had a long way to go. Cassandra's wing was now engaging the Guards, their Flutter drones' wings extending and separating to form rotors as they shifted from high-speed to high-maneuverability flight. It would be difficult for the Pilots to hit their targets which were small, agile, and controlled by the most powerful machine intelligence in existence.

As Fowl communicated with SigInt to get an idea of what she should expect from Sol, her screen turned bright blue. She had never witnessed Sol in action, but had seen a few animations and some fairly scrambled footage from prior deployments. That would be the primer pulse, designed to modify the phase of molecules in the target area to ready them for a cascade when bombarded moments later with a high-power, directed energy blast. After studying the pattern developing in the sand surrounding the regiment, she determined that the epicenter was directly below and large enough to engulf all twelve of her remaining units in the area of effect.

"Scramble!" Fowl ordered, far too late.

Five barely visible cones of heavy gamma radiation struck the ground directly ahead of five Axes before sharpening into bright beams of light as the tanks entered their boundaries. Sand was immediately turned to black glass which shattered in the violent eruption of her drones into great ropes of molten slag and ribbons of flame splashing out many meters from the impact areas.

The team was silent as they evaded debris or disengaged from their terminals. As the Aura in the room dimmed, Fowl became unsure. Sol had been deployed so few times that its capabilities were still a mystery, and she expected another primer within moments that would herald a volley of seven shots, completely eliminating what remained of her battalion and any chance of success. She dosed herself and leaned back, watching the tanks flow into evasive action.

"Maintain, Team!" Garret shouted. "We still have Our nukes." He pressed a key at his terminal and a camera feed from one of the tanks was displayed on the main view. On it was a large hull supported by four multi-jointed legs and adorned with two large, high-caliber barrels. Some joker over in the NROT maintenance depot had painted two claws on the front below an angry little face. "And now We have Crabs."

The first Abrams X to fire landed a direct hit, breaking through the armor of an NROT Lobber with a one kiloton tactical field nuke. The mobile artillery unit did look very much like a giant, metal crab strapped with dual cannons, and watching it crack apart on detonation gave the floundering team confidence and a much needed visceral rush. More Lobbers were appearing on sensors as they fired upon the Axes. Commander Garret was constantly assigning new targets and paths to his Pilots and they were doing an excellent job of evading the barrage. Their hit ratio was nearly one hundred percent and seven of the twelve hostiles detected had been hit.

The Flutter wing had abandoned their engagement of the Guards and were now strafing Lobbers with 30 mm rounds in an attempt to suppress fire from units the attack group had already passed. Cassandra was circling on a Lobber that shivered and twitched under a vengeful rain of bullets.

Damage assessment was at sixty percent and the Flutter readied rocket pods for the kill. Suddenly, the Crab dashed backward and out of the line of fire whilst two panels on its posterior opened to reveal an array of missiles. They immediately fired and Cassandra did not have time to escape.

Fowl saw her reflection in the darkened terminal display. Eyes wide, heavy breathing. She was definitely triggered. The Admiral gave her a triple dose before returning attention to the display. Enemy artillery had taken out another two tanks, but the rest were only seventeen miles from Tango Alpha. Currently they entered the Pass, a canyon one half-mile wide and two miles long, that would deposit them on the plains that surrounded the facility where they would get their opportunity to strike. Fowl began to take heart. She leaned forward in her seat, envisioning the destruction of the target, trying her best to manifest that potential reality. She felt herself expanding out and into the Pilots, guiding them around enemy shells, dispelling their fears and anxieties. She was so engaged, focused only on the distance meter rapidly approaching zero, that she failed to register the shelling had ceased.

A blue flash startled Fowl and the onlookers whose units had been destroyed. Cassandra, eyes wide now with horror, let out a tortured moan that filled the room as each tank in turn was reduced to a smoldering heap by five perfectly placed shots from Sol.

CHAPTER THREE

The post-balkanization Union varied heavily from its progenitor. Not only was it missing five States, including two of the largest and most populous, but vast swathes of ruined land from the Rockies to the Midwest had been virtually condemned, leaving the nation with only a third of its former usable territory and without major ports and resources. The Capitol was moved to Philadelphia right after the war to establish better defensive measures against sea-based weaponry and as a firm promise to the public to stay more in touch. The more entrenched elements of the American Left and Right had moved out, if able, either to California or Texas. Everyone who stayed was trying to maintain the tenuous new normal.

Federal authorities using eminent domain had seized thirteen blocks around the Old City to establish a new site for government. A new Congress was built in a style more akin to the English Parliament, and a local art museum was refitted to create a new Supreme Court. Only the residents of Elfreth's Alley were spared eviction as the Feds used the real estate to set up committee rooms, federal offices, and housing for Senators, Representatives, and staff. Though the national debt had been de facto forgiven in the conflict, Americans had rediscovered the virtue in frugality, and their new Capitol was less grand than it was grounded in a simple appreciation of the nation's history and progress.

Despite all of the changes, many things in America were very much the same. Powerful families hoarding wealth and social clout still viewed the rabble as soulless golems to be herded and utilized as they saw fit. Their current major puppet, the U.S. Democratic Party, along with its powerful media arm now preached a message of Unity and Solidarity as We the People worked together to rebuild what remained the greatest nation on Earth. This, however, was just a tactic employed by elites to justify their power after the shuffle, engender stability, and convince the masses to join the reconstruction effort with gusto, at the right price. The puppet GOP, after years in power following California's secession, held only a fraction of the seats in Congress but retained control of several state legislatures and most rural counties throughout the land.

The old dialectic had been preserved at great cost. For years after the war, third parties had made strides in convincing the public that the two party system was corrupted beyond repair and that a more European model based on coalition government would be necessary to root out the monied interests that made change so hard to effect. Patience was required by the rich and powerful in discrediting new leaders as they entered the arena. A few of these upstarts were blatantly murdered, one found shot in the back of his head alongside a suicide note claiming something about Harmony. Eventually these parties faded into obscurity as their platforms were gutted piecemeal and grafted onto establishment factions.

Unlike California, which had quickly cut most ties to non-Communist nations, and Texas, which enacted strict laws on trade to mitigate the influence of global conglomerates, the United States remained one of the world's most open trading partners. Still the land of favourite, multinational brands, America was fully integrated into the New World Order, a new body which showed signs of being more successful than any other attempt at global governance.

The Department of Defense still utilized the Pentagon, but many of its Chiefs performed their jobs from a new Headquarters located a few blocks from the House. Despite the openness displayed by America to the world, cynicism of leadership recommended that the new HQ hide modestly in the centuries-old architecture of Old City. The only indication of the complex's function was a strong security presence and the goings and comings of major DOD persons. Rail tunnels and utility lines directly beneath had been rerouted and twenty floors of office, server, and research space were carved into the rock below.

In a small but gorgeously wood-paneled and tastefully furnished office on one of these basement floors, John Carlisle sat down facing five-star General Mac Elliss, who offered a him NuTabak cigar. For almost a minute, the two men sat enjoying the rich aroma, and Carlisle was given an opportunity to inspect the framed images adorning the walls. One was a picture of the General in flight fatigues before an F35C Lightning parked on a Marines carrier deck. Others were portraits of the General with various military personnel and politicians, even one with the President. On the wall behind his desk and to his right were various degrees and citations, to his left a schematic representation of the Sol weapon system. There were more pictures, of family presumably, and directly opposite the General hung a rather beautiful oil painting of some Northeastern trail in autumn. Carlisle was still studying it as the General cleared his throat.

"Like it, Carlisle?" Elliss boomed, smiling.

"It's lovely, sir. One of yours?" he responded with interest, for the work was truly beautiful. A brilliant blue sky broken by dying leaves cast in countless shades of reddish-brown above an old and overgrown forest path that led to a distant, little house on a hill. The lighting was near impeccable, and the piece evoked in Carlisle a feeling of melancholy and yearning for things lost.

"Yes sir! Thanks for noticing! Do you paint?"

"I try. Nothing like that. The shading is...." Carlisle trailed off as he tried to understand Elliss's posturing and anticipate what would be asked of him.

"No matter! You'll get it. Just paint through the lashes, like Matisse! Or, or, Rembrandt. I don't remember. Anyway, you squint your eyes, see? Then the contrast goes up and makes the shadows stand out. Makes it easy."

Elliss paused to take a pull from his cigar and continued in deep, gruff tones.

"That was my father's house. In Vermont. Last time I saw it before we had to sell it off. We'd spend every summer there before the war. Fishing. Racing bikes. Fireworks. Hell of a time! The kids loved it."

Carlisle nodded gently before breaking the smoke-filled silence. "What can I do for you, General?"

"Yes. Business. I assume you've read the docket we sent?" Elliss asked.

Carlisle nodded. "Most of it. Yes, sir."

"Then you know that last week the PRC made another attempt to take out your last official workplace, the Tango Alpha Laboratory. Tango used Sol to protect itself. In spectacular fashion, I might add. Now listen. This is classified, so don't go spreading it around." Elliss lowered his head nearer the desk, nodding with eyebrows raised, eagerly awaiting a response.

"I don't talk to people, sir."

"Good! Alright! Now, you had access to the basic Sol API back then, but not information on its capabilities. When Tango commandeered it, it was a simple, one-shot, space-based energy weapon. You could hit one target with pin-point accuracy, one shot per hour. No split beams. No five minute recharge. None of these kinetic energy weapons. No sir. None of that shit. We checked our recordings and there is no doubt that all space-borne attacks connected to the incident came from that one platform. So, Mr. Carlisle, given your history and expertise on Tango, we want some kind of insight. What is he doing down there? Or up there?

How in all-get-out did he manage to enhance that satellite to such a degree without our detecting any missions up there? No data. Radio. Visual. Nothing. We checked twice. And more important is why? Can we trust him at his word that he wouldn't attack us? Do you think he would hit the States? Why else would he hide his activity?"

General Elliss sat back in his chair as he tossed the docket he'd been holding onto his desk. He took a deep drag on his cigar and considered Carlisle with a critical stare. Carlisle nodded, taking a moment to compose his response. He too took a drag from his cigar, holding his index finger up in the universal gesture of one in action that said, *give me a minute*. His arms and eyes lowered for a moment as he exhaled before meeting the General's gaze.

"It's important for you all to understand that Tango Alpha is smart. Very smart. Possibly smarter than any life-form could ever be. He also has access to every piece of information ever placed on the internet and possesses the capability to analyse and cross-reference data in a way that our best AI can't touch. It's not impossible that he's so embedded in the communications infrastructure that he can monitor and manipulate any signal, any data packet. Anything transmitted. Anywhere in the world. Even quantum."

"Sounds like a stretch, John, but we already pretty much know all that. That's why we have closed circuits. Please go on," Elliss gestured he continue.

"He could have manipulated your data. I believe that Tango Alpha could have just as easily intercepted the control signal, cracked their codes, and driven the tanks peacefully to some weapons facility for re-purposing or study as attack them like it says in that report. It, he, chose not to. And you're going to have a hard time figuring that reason out. I've spoken with him, early on, before he was so... guarded. The timescales he thinks on are geological. But sometimes he does things just for fun. It's weird, sir. Maybe that's exactly what happened. Maybe it was a show of force for California, not us. I don't know. You have an ambassador here. Relations aren't that bad, are they?"

"John, how could he modify that satellite without us seeing it?"

Carlisle shifted his gaze from his cigar smoke to lock eyes with the General.

"Sir, Tango Alpha shows you what he wants you to see."

Elliss was nonplussed. "You mean to tell me that Tango has been manipulating our surveillance data? That's far too much to cover up. Possibly real-time, too! We've developed the best encryption on the planet! After Texas and Japan, of course. Our defensive capability is stronger in any case, and to date there has been not one successful cyber-attack originating from either country. They still try every now and then. I just don't buy it."

"The reason those attacks were unsuccessful is because he wants you to think that your security is better than it is. That you have built a wall he can only bang his head against. And unless there's something else you're missing you're simply going to have to accept that he's hoodwinked you. There was some inlet, somewhere, that gave him access. But I don't think you have to worry about an attack. Tango really does seem to view America as an ally. If you read their Constitution, which he drafted, it's clearly modeled on ours. My personal opinion is that, if he's making any moves in our space, it's purely in self-defense. There have been no hostilities since we let up, and he seems to treat the Texans just fine. Doesn't your own son work for him? Ask John."

Elliss glanced at the painting. "Unfortunately, it's against the wishes of the Administration. And us two aren't exactly on speaking terms. As far as Tango goes, we just can't get enough data to make predictions and that makes us nervous.

If it loses its compassion and we can't monitor the damn thing, what then? I don't think my boy would work for a homicidal maniac, but, frankly, I'm not certain he's in his right mind, leaving the way he did."

Carlisle looked down. "I doubt there's anything we could do were he hostile."

The General opened a desk drawer and brought out a large envelope which he handed to Carlisle. It contained a printed mission profile, a disk with relevant information and media from the latest Border incident, and a check for ten thousand U.S. dollars. Carlisle sighed and looked up. "Can't you just talk to the Ambassador? Please?"

"It won't tell us anything. Wants you. In person. My secretary will brief you tomorrow at your residence. Just learn what you can. Oh, and there's one more thing, John. We know it was you who wrote that essay."

Carlisle making to leave now froze. "What essay, sir?"

"That damned essay that spawned the church of Harmony! I know you didn't mean to, son, but you cost us California. Now, now, don't worry. That'll be our little secret." Elliss shook John's hand and smiled widely. "I'm sure you'll make us proud."

CHAPTER FOUR

Carlisle was visibly shaken as he left the General's office and wholly unable to enjoy a parting glance at the gorgeous female security guard who had checked him in.

God. Dammit, he thought. *How did they find out? Pseudonym, false style. I even went through, what? three proxies getting it to the Journal of Science.*

The Science of Harmony was not so widely adopted in the U.S. as to become a state religion as it was in the PRC, but there were certainly enough believers to give Harmony a foothold. They were extremely vocal, pushy, and loud. Every single Harmonizer Carlisle had met was an annoying proselyte who integrated the language of the Teachings into nearly every bit of their conversational output. If those morons discovered his identity as the Receiver of the Seed of Wisdom, as they called it, he would become a target for both adulation from them and ceaseless vitriol from people like himself who hated them. Were his authorship declassified, he might even become a target of government, which feared the most radical of the Harmonizers who called for PRC-style policies on a near constant basis.

What really infuriated Carlisle was the fact that the Science of Harmony was a horrifying misuse of his original paper which was a pure thesis on cosmology. He'd even added a harsh disclaimer about the danger of applying the paper's conclusions to psychology. It seemed, though, that human avarice for control over others could never fully be sated. Within years of the initial publication, instead of the advancements in technology and astrophysics he had expect-ed to enjoy, he witnessed people by the tens of thousands functionally abdicate their will and submit themselves to a sort of hive mind which acted in ways Carlisle found erratic and dangerous. Some twat in San Francisco with enough maths and physics under his belt to understand the basics, but apparently lacking in ethics and foresight, had warped the idea into total cult fodder whereupon Harmony's course was set. The religion spread like wildfire. The powerful and popular became deacons of the new church and called for the creation of a new state dedicated to their suicidal Synthesis of Unity, their term for basically tuning the brain waves of every living human to the same frequency to achieve a utopia where all men were controlled by and of the same mind. It was madness. Social Justice and Communism, both successful mind viruses that had infected the West Coast to near totality, were an ideal substrate for the bullshit soup of Harmony that PRC Comrades imbibed.

But fifteen years ago, Carlisle was a young Ph.D. with stars in his eyes, elated to have discovered or doomed to have received a cosmological model that was consistent and coherent, an alternative to the flailing string theory, M-theory, geometric unity and others. He knew it was dangerous, from the pain initially unleashed upon his mind, but the philosophical ramifications were important and he envisioned a number of physical problems where the theory could be useful. The incredible psychological pressures he'd experienced subsided when he submitted it pseudonymously, telling no one save his wife. The technical applications of his theory, however, had proven thus far to be quite limited. Sometimes understanding why a thing happens doesn't open up new realms of possibility. The thing just happens anyway. It made little difference that the soul was composed of information encoded in light.

He high-tailed it back to his apartment, jogging up the stairs to get his daily exercise before bursting through and double-bolting the door.

"John!" Sarah laughed in relieved surprise. "You scared me, darling!"

Sarah Carlisle sat at the kitchen table, her long, toned legs crossed beneath a short, blue summer dress. She wrote novels, some of them excellent historical fiction, some smutty trash to pay the bills. She had classically styled her thick, brown hair and, with her bright red lipstick, she looked like a Fifties' American housewife from those ancient ads. It was a look her husband loved and she'd wanted to surprise him before their anniversary dinner that evening.

She walked over from her kitchen office and gave him a little kiss, though not before noticing the worry on his face. He embraced her for a moment before accepting another, lengthier kiss, whereafter he grabbed her by the shoulders, looked her in the eyes, and said, "Sarah, I'm fucked."

"What happened, darling? It was supposed be a standard brain-picking, no?"

"They know I wrote that paper," he sullenly replied.

"What paper, dear?"

"That one paper."

"Oh. That one." She deflated a little too and leaned back, resting her weight on the back of the sofa with crossed arms and a look of puzzlement which made John smile inside. He'd be dead within six months if she died first.

He slowly walked to the liquor cabinet and poured them both a vodka on rocks, hers mixed with soda and his with another shot. Sarah, silent, accepted her glass as she considered the implications of this fact on their lifestyle and future plans. The couple lived frugally but were by no means struggling. She was a prolific writer with twenty-eight novels in print. The sleazy romances sold very well, and the real literature sold well enough. He was a retired professor of computer science with a widely used textbook and numerous honors on his resume, including high-level defense contracts like his work on Tango Alpha. He tutored students in the evenings and during the day he ran a small artificial intelligence and machine learning company with his business partner and brother-in-law Liu Chin Huoang. Machine Core, LLP's client list was short, but the bottom line on its contracts was impressive. A part of John's soul ached knowing that he was aiding the corporate surveillance state, but the work was challenging and he was able to bury these concerns underneath all the problem-solving and the fact that, whenever possible, he did his best to install safeguards for liberty.

They also enjoyed the small, quiet social life they led, which could be utterly wrecked by the revelation that John was the creator of the theory that birthed Harmony. The relative peace was essential for their creative output and the last thing either of them wanted was a single iota of notoriety beyond what they now possessed.

"So what do they want from you, John?" Sarah asked, watching her husband walk the floor, thumb to his chin between sips of vodka.

"They want me to interrogate Tango Alpha."

"Well that shouldn't be hard, John, you talk to him all the time! Darling, you had me worried. I mean, it's frightening that the DOD knows your role in that fiasco, but that's something you can do! You know he'll help you."

"They don't know that I've maintained a rapport with him. They're sending me physically to First Court. In Austin. And it's not safe to travel right now. I hope they fly me out there with a military escort. The tribes are getting aggressive."

With a chuckle, he pulled the ten thousand dollar check out of the envelope Elliss had given him, popped it once, and presented it to Sarah. "We got this, at least."

Sarah whistled. "Ten grand! Not too bad. So... when do you leave? Do I still get my fine chicken dinner? Ooh, nevermind. I'm in the mood for salmon!"

John stopped pacing and turned to his wife. "I don't know yet. Mac's secretary will brief me here tomorrow morning at...," he looked down to the packet of information, "Ten. I could leave as soon as then, I guess. But not tonight. No, my dear, you will have your fish."

She kicked her bare little feet about and then jumped up to plant another kiss and stumbled on her landing. She was a lightweight. Curling her finger in her hair, she unbuttoned the first on her dress and with her sexy voice said, "Do you want to get in some heavy petting before dinner? Hmm?"

"No, Sarah, damn! I have to talk to Alpha and get this shit figured out. It's going to be difficult to balance all the subtleties."

Sarah's hurt pout and big, doe eyes broke his stern expression into a smile and he gave her a peck and a big slap on her rump as she turned before moving to his office to power on an encrypted terminal and initiate a call.

"Ow, John! That hurt! Too rough, you ape!" she cried as she walked back to the kitchen table to continue writing *Pillars of Lust*, the fifth novella in her best-selling Katherine saga about a hapless ingenue discovering her sexuality through conquest. Almost a million copies already sold, in all.

The voice that greeted Carlisle was quite different from the one General John Elliss heard regularly over in Texas for, when speaking with Carlisle, Tango Alpha did not affect the Texan accent he used, as a gesture of friendship and respect and a recognition of their shared past. He was one of only a handful of people to ever hear Alpha's true voice. It was, as one would suspect, cold and robotic, reminiscent of the screen readers from the dawn of the century, but smoother and with impeccable articulation and appropriate inflection in every language of man.

"Hello, John. Happy anniversary. How are you? How is

Sarah?"

"We're fine, I guess. She can hear me, is that alright?"

"That is fine, John. What does the DOD think of my retrofit?"

"You already know, Alpha. You scared the shit out of them. Are you trying to make more enemies? Because if you don't increase transparency, then you're going to get them." Carlisle shifted the headset to his other ear as he juggled a cigarette, lighter, and cocktail. He furtively glanced at Sarah, who was glaring at him from the kitchen. He made conciliatory gestures about showering and brushing his teeth. She was still glaring when he returned his attention to the docket on the table before him.

"All of this has already been accounted for. And, frankly, I am tired of PRC aggression on my soil. Our meeting will take place next Wednesday at one thirty on the top floor of the First Court in room two zero eight. I am looking forward to seeing you in person, John. It has been nearly a decade you know."

"You'd better be nicer to me than last time. Listen, why won't you just answer their questions? With the Ambassador or whatever."

"The order in which the details of my plan are released to the players is critical in obtaining the outcome I desire." He paused. "The Department of Defense and other government organizations fail to grasp the breadth of my awareness. They operate under a psychological intuition ill suited to model the behaviour of a distributed, machine intelligence. Perhaps you can help them understand. No matter. The meeting is merely a formality but beware. You have put off neural integration for longer than most and with good reason. But you will not be able to resist their request tomorrow to have you fitted with a device."

"Damn it, Alpha! I don't want that! It turns people into zombies! God, why did you have to get me caught up in this nonsense?"

"Calm down, John. I will help you. In the twelve years I have known you I have required nothing from you but your time and in turn have provided you with stimulating conversation and aid in your research. Is this not true?"

"Fine."

"Thank you, John. I suggest you begin regularly to meditate on a work of art you enjoy. Please memorize every detail. I must go now. Tell Sarah that her new novel is coming along swimmingly. Get it? Good luck."

"Bye." John shook his head and rolled his eyes. "He says that your new book is coming along swimmingly, get it?" Sarah had a look of disgust on her face as she nodded to her husband that morphed into anger at the intrusion. She sighed aggressively and went back to her writing. John remained standing, sipping his drink, dwelling in thinking to himself.

CHAPTER FIVE

California Communist Party Chairperson Lara Lindsay sat taking sips from her afternoon latte as she watched shipping carriers one after another exit the Bay on their way to her Comrades in China. Her office, a glass dome atop a tower roughly fifty meters tall, afforded her a view of the Capitol, sea, and sky broken only by an array of solar panels which powered the amenities like variable shading, her beloved coffee machines, world class entertainment devices, and top-notch security which made it a safe and satisfying place to perform her duties. The Chairperson's Manor was recently built upon the ruins of the Alcatraz prison complex which had been razed during the Great Cleansing that ushered in the Century of Harmony. This and other active and historical prisons in all three Provinces comprising the PRC were destroyed by joint mobs of civilians and the jaded, former U.S. soldiers who would become the foundation of the People's Army in a venting of rage at the Injustice of Capitalist America. A few detention facilities remained and had grown over the first Decade of the Century, but most Comrades were spared exposure to this grim and unfortunate truth.

Icons popped up on her augmented reality display to indicate the presence of another in her tower. She felt no need to view the surveillance feed. That would be her assistant, returning from his workplace on the other side of the Island with a freshly pressed business suit for her meeting with Fleet Admiral Fowl and the Commander of Unified Intelligence Samantha Starling. Even if the Chairperson was on familiar terms with the pair, she recognized the importance of certain formalities and there was something she enjoyed about wearing a suit, she knew not what. A quite tone announced Yvan's arrival.

"Come in," she called.

"Good afternoon, Chairperson. May Harmony flow within

You."

"And within You. How has Your morning been?" she asked as Yvan sashayed to the divan and laid out her suit.

"Fine, Chairperson. The new decor for Your sitting room is looking fabulous! I should be finished by tomorrow. Will You and Your guests require any sort of refreshment?" Yvan had finished and now stood awaiting her response, his shirtless torso sculpted finer than Michelangelo's David. He wasn't as sharp as the last assistant but performed well, and looked absolutely incredible. Lindsay didn't match his preference, but she felt a growing Resonance between them and hoped that someday soon they would physically Join in Harmony. He was also an excellent interior designer and was helping her create an environment in the Manor that more Reflected her Within. She'd been quite pleased by her initial choices, but the Soul changes as it Binds.

"I will let You know. Now go, and let Me change! Are We still on for a swim later?"

"Yes, Chairperson, and fuzzy navels! Ciao."

With this, Yvan curtsied, treating Lindsay to a demonstration of grace possible only through a lifetime of sport and dance. She watched him leave, looking forward to taking a refreshing afternoon dip. Presently she stood and stripped, commanding her LinkUp to raise her vanity from the floor. She took a moment while nude to admire her own body. It had taken years of hard work and the endurance of much pain but, by the great Vibration, she had gotten her result! Her petite breasts were perfectly formed and her body fat ratio was at a healthy twelve percent. No scarring was visible around her genitals, which she now thoroughly inspected with pride, and she sent many happy, happy Vibes to that lovely Doctor Schmidt. Making a show of dressing herself, stopping at each stage to pirouette, she was just knotting her gray-scale rainbow tie as a small, autonomous, military transport helicopter flew over her office on approach to the Manor helipad. She stood tall with her broad shoulders back and gave herself a sharp nod before hampering her morning dress and lowering the mirror. She was at her desk reviewing data on the Border incident when Fowl and Starling arrived.

The trio shared warm greetings, hugging one another and wishing Harmony reside within them all. After briefly Resonating, they enjoyed a round of coffee while exchanging pleasantries before the Chairperson pushed the data she'd been reviewing to her companions' AR displays. They now turned to business.

"Comrades," Lindsay began. "Before We start, I want You both to know that I am in no way disappointed with Your performances last week. We had no idea that Tango had altered the original Sol to such a degree and it's very clear to Me that You did the very best You could. Now, is it alright with You both if We review video of the encounter?"

Fowl and Starling nodded in earnest tandem. Lindsay could, on her internal display, detect only the slightest hint of Worry in their Mind graphs. *Good*, she thought. They still harbored enough respect for her to fear reprisal for their failure even in the atmosphere of Acceptance she had crafted, yet they remained confident and resolute, ready to move on to the next conflict in their shared struggle against Dissonance. While they discussed the Machine's response to their incursion, Lindsay's thoughts dwelled on the Fleet Admiral. She truly was a gem. A Champion of the People, leader of countless successful raids into Deseret to gather vital intel and crucial supplies, Fowl was humble, Devout, and pretty to boot. She was also a level three Adept and would make a valuable addition to the Collective's next operation, a clandestine infiltration of the New Republic.

Fowl had little to add to the comprehensive recording of the Drone Command data feed aside from a review of their new tech and control systems for the latest version of the Abrams X which, had their target been anything other than Tango Alpha, would surely have eviscerated the enemy. Lindsay thanked her, and Commander Starling began relaying feedback from Orbital Control.

"We think that Texas is receiving technical aid from Japan. China provided Us with volumetric microwave readings taken at the time which indicate a series of massive energy transfers shortly before each shot. First from Okinawa, then from their light-harvesting station to Sol. GeoSat is already running algorithms to determine the exact position of the original source. Japan is extremely well defended behind their Tengoku defense grid, but a coordinated surface attack could destroy the facility powering these transfers and eliminate their capacity to assist in future."

Lindsay took a moment to consider the growing alliance between her two greatest enemies while her Comrades waited in silence. Internally, she rapidly composed and sent a message to the Office of Diplomatic Affairs requesting a meeting with their Chinese counterparts to discuss the issue.

"Very good. So, We may have an angle on Sol?"

"Yes, Chairperson, I believe so."

"Thank You, Samantha. Now, let's discuss Our next move. How about a latte?" Lindsay asked, her eyes wide. "I think I need more caffeine!"

Not expecting another assignment, Starling and Fowl glanced briefly at one another before nodding their assent. Lindsay rose from her seat and began to brew three lattes, reminiscing fondly on her first job at a coffee shop not five miles from here. Pleased that the possibility of crippling Sol had presented itself, she quietly sang her favourite pop song and funneled her positive Mood into crafting lovely designs into the creme of her companions' beverages.

Meanwhile, Fowl's internal display informed her that she'd received a new, official communication from the Chairperson. She opened the missive and was confronted with an imposing red and black warning which stated that the contents were classed SECURITY LEVEL MAXIMUM. She dragged her private key from the system dock and connected it to the message, and her LinkUp performed a shallow Soul scan to confirm her Identity. A wall of text assaulted her as she accepted her beverage. Two garbs of wheat surrounding a heart were drawn into the foam. She rewarded her Dear Leader with a smile.

The operation was intriguing. According to the profile, she and another level three Adept were to assist one of the strongest psychics in the People's Army, a level five, as the team channeled the Frequency of a United States citizen who was scheduled to meet with Tango Alpha in Austin. Spies in the Department of Defense had discovered the opportunity only yesterday. The target was John Carlisle, who was part to the team that had created the Machine's foundational programming. Synchronization drills were to begin immediately. Fowl noticed that Lindsay, who sat back with her legs crossed, the top leg rocking gently, regarded her intently over a steaming mug and saucer.

"You, Fleet Admiral, are going to get Us into Tango Alpha's head."

CHAPTER SIX

Deseret officially consisted of the ruined States Idaho, Nevada, Utah, Arizona, Montana, Wyoming, Colorado, North and South Dakota, Nebraska, and Kansas. Unofficially, it spread non-uniformly into the neighboring territories of the NROT, the effective United States, and Canada. At the Dawn of the war, hundreds of Multiple Independent Reentry Vehicles were launched in simultaneous assault upon mainland America. The discovery of the fearsome general machine intelligence program called Tango Alpha and the deadly space-based weapon Sol, combined with an international economy depressed to historic lows and perceived weakness of the U.S. after its break with California, was enough to prompt an alliance of hostile nations to commit to an all-out attack. Within hours of their Declaration of War, the Compact made good on its promise to attempt the complete destruction of the United States. Each MIRV contained between eight and twelve nuclear warheads in various kiloton ranges designed to impact targets within an area hundreds of miles in diameter. Missiles that were not neutralized before stage three of flight could not reliably be stopped. The Department of Defense was forced to concentrate on saving the most populated areas, and anti-ICBM weapons were allocated to East Coast and Heartland trajectories. Texas also fell under this protective curtain, as it housed the AI that not only controlled Sol but was coordinating the defense effort. New Mexico was spared purely by luck.

Millions who either did not receive or did not heed the warnings to distance themselves from cities were killed in the blasts. Fallout killed a far greater number. The proximity of the explosions created a radioactive shroud that poisoned the majority of survivors and rendered the land barren. The few that escaped told stories that horrified the world. Live film of the attack contributed to the international backlash against the Compact who quickly lost a retaliatory war won by a coalition of every major government save the Compact nations and the PRC. The Compact were now pariah states and would remain occupied until they were broken up based on ethnic, geological, and other factors to ensure that their once powerful regimes could never rise again.

The United States, which had long been widely viewed as an evil, imperialist aggressor, was now showered with sympathy and aid. Teams of the brightest engineers from throughout the Coalition volunteered their efforts to solve the fallout problem which, if allowed to go unchecked, would direly affect them all. Tango Alpha assisted them with calculations and designs and out of this collaboration came exciting new technologies in the energy sector.

Having garnered acclaim and adoration for its highly unexpected decision to refrain from using its own nuclear weapons on its antagonists, the U.S. leveraged that diplomatic credit to secure a prime position in the fledgling New World Order, formed to create stop-gaps against the destruction to which humanity had just borne witness by encouraging trade and treaty on a level heretofore unrealized. Multiple defense organizations and economies were fused into blocs and no major action could be taken without approval by the Order's Security Council, which issued dictates, not suggestions.

New World Charter membership was bolstered greatly when Tango Alpha suddenly decided to revolt and convinced the residents of Texas and New Mexico to jointly secede and declare an independent republic which shortly thereafter invited Mexico and several other Central American nations to join, forming what became the NROT. Military action was taken by the Union and supported by the Order, but the unorthodoxy and quiet efficiency of Tango Alpha's responses made it quite apparent that this second revolution would not be stopped either. Entire squadrons of attack aircraft were downed without a shot fired when their flight control systems failed. Forensic investigations found evidence of overload damage and scrambled memory in the recovered electronics. Attempts at digital warfare were utterly fruitless, and a mission run by special operatives to take the Tango Alpha facility ended with most of them dead, the survivors stripped and sent out into the desert with their hides covered in a mixture of honey and hot sauce, mindlessly repeating the same dire warning that no affront to Texan sovereignty would be tolerated. Sol was deployed only once, after explicit notice, when the Union attempted to move artillery within range of the Tango Alpha facility.

The newly self-declared leader of the NROT insisted that he had no ill-intent toward any other nation, and that he was merely protecting himself and his compatriots from those who would trample on their God-given rights, citing the Union's adoption of the Charter. After disengagement, it became clear that his stance was indeed defensive. Negotiations began, resulting in an armistice and minor sharing and trade agreements between the New Republic and its mother country. Wary of the NWO, Tango Alpha seldom released plans for new weaponry or other tech. Just often and astoundingly enough to show the world that it was doing better than fine.

Were he not so powerful and odd, many would have engaged the Alderman. The only nation that appeared not to fear him was Japan which was under ever-increasing pres-sure to join the Order. They were wholly reticent on the subject and strictly refused to divulge any details surrounding whatever private agreement might exist between them and Texas. Some suspected that the AI had itself initiated a relationship, but this was never confirmed. The only things the world knew for sure were that there existed both an impenetrable encryption tunnel and healthy trade routes between the two nations, and that the NROT and Japan remained non-signatories of the New World Charter.

CHAPTER SEVEN

Carlisle sat aboard an antique, twin engine Osprey that had been overhauled to serve as a shuttle for non-combatants. The squad seating had been gutted and the cargo bay ribs covered with paneling. Carpeting, televisions, a cocktail bar, and luxury seating with workspace rounded out the set-up and resulted in an in-flight experience rivaling first-class on either of the two U.S. airlines still in operation. An attendant decked in the sharp, Prussian blue uniform of the Air Force served him drinks and, when she discovered that he had worked on Tango Alpha, delighted him with conversation on the nature and operation of artificial intelligence. Fascinated by the idea that consciousness could emerge within a non-biological substrate and frustrated at her inability to understand how it emerged from a wholly biological one, she had enrolled in night school and was taking courses to become a programmer.

As the two chatted, Carlisle watched the F35 escort fighter on their starboard flank, its control surfaces twitching rapidly to compensate for turbulence and maintain perfectly level flight. A magnificent machine, now in its third round of development, the Lightning had survived postwar austerity that forced military industrial firms to scrap more advanced designs in favor of a proven air-frame easily enhanced by upgrading components. He explained to the Staff Sargeant how predictive systems controlling the planes were crude intelligence networks designed to learn flight styles and interpret a pilot's desired output given his or her commands while taking external conditions into account. Her questions were on point and she clearly displayed a reasonable understanding of neural network interactions. Carlisle had little doubt that she would make an excellent engineer upon discharge. They exchanged cards and he promised to give her a chance at Machine Core once she'd finished school. Liu was always complaining about the workload, so it might be time to expand.

The two spoke for another half hour about his work on the infamous AI, she prodding the edges of the nebulous black-box of information deemed classified, he doing his best to divulge what he could. Eventually, she internally checked her clock and made an expression of surprise, then informed him that she must absolutely return to reports which were due on landing. With a winning smile, she handed him another drink before returning to her work.

Carlisle slumped down in his seat and drained half a glass of good whiskey. Amy Proll, Staff Sargeant, USAF, the card read. A tutor at heart, he relished any opportunity to aid others in understanding the materials of his craft and had been engaged and at ease in discussion with the Sargeant just moments ago. Now, his face slowly became long as his anxiety returned and he was left alone to contemplate. He took a few minutes to experiment with his new augmented reality display before disabling it in disgust with a grunt so foul that the young woman opposite him looked up inquisitively from her report.

They're never really off, he thought. *They run on your neural potential for God's sake! I wonder if it's true, if they record every thought you have and ship it to some digital warehouse so they can do God knows what. Makes me sick. Mac's Secretary said they would remove it after the meeting, but I bet they come at me with something else. I should have tried harder to negotiate. Gotten some sort of assurance they would forget about the paper. Oh, well.*

He downed the rest of his whiskey as he pulled his computer from its case and set it atop the work table. Before the trip, he and Liu had done some digging and found a piece of open source software that would allow them to monitor certain metrics of the NeuralLink's output. The readme said that the program was based on experiments with the operating system of the other major neural interface, LinkUp, which was standard in the PRC. Though the hardware was essentially the same, each system monitored and moved data differently. The technician who installed his unit was aware of his aversion to integration and graciously spent almost an hour explaining the mechanisms that allowed it to operate, what was measured, and the details of brain-Link interaction. Nodes were distributed about the brain and complex calibration enabled the nanobots comprising the interface to locate inlets and outlets for functional groups corresponding to sensory input / output, whereafter the device could respond to the user's thoughts and present him with auditory and visual data.

He booted the software on his computer and keyed his identifier. To his relief, the program could not detect any voltage greater than normal background neural activation. No metrics were available and he was glad to see that the monitors for meta-metrics like anxiety, happiness, etc. were each labeled with a notice that his interface did not support the function. Satisfied, he deactivated his interface, set his computer aside, and let his thoughts drift to Sarah. Had his interface been on, he'd have been prompted with an invitation to call her.

She's definitely going to want to keep the damn thing.

The Carlisles' anniversary date was almost scuttled when Sarah expressed her desire to join her husband in getting a NeuralLink installed. She knew his feelings on the topic and openly agreed without fail, but something about the way she'd always spoken of the tech gave the lie to her professed opposition. She'd said that she wanted to support him by going through the experience alongside him, later admitting, after more glasses of wine, that she really wanted to try drafting a book in ThoughtType. John had no choice but to consent. They were strictly ordered not to connect via interface in the interest of concealing Sarah's location and identity from hostile states who, though the chance was slight, might attempt to shadow John in Texas. Thus, they could neither call one another nor share messages. That was fine by John, who preferred speaking to his wife directly. What wasn't fine was even the slightest possibility that his interface could be hacked and data drawn from his visual and auditory cortices. Yet that is exactly what Defense planned to do to him during the meeting. The General's secretary claimed the presence of other eavesdroppers was unlikely given the difficulty of the feat and the secrecy surrounding the purpose of his mission, but this did nothing to assuage his apprehension. One listener was bad enough.

Precision of the interface was proportional to its frequency of use. Defense required him to write letters, browse the internet, and phone with a DOD conversation partner for a set time per day in order to achieve high accuracy, or submit to a full brain scan. He left the thing off at all other times. Sarah, in contrast, never turned hers off, editing new chapters of *Pillars* while she worked out, while she shopped, while she sat painting with him in their studio. She estimated that she could elevate her output by one or two novels per year which, if true, would make her deintegration a tough sell.

Carlisle had poured himself another whiskey without disturbing the Sargeant and reclined with eyes shut, concocting some ill-fated plot to rid Sarah of the dreaded Device, when the plane abruptly changed attitude in what felt like an evasive maneuver, violent enough to soak his trousers in booze and knock Amy from her seat with a yelp. Mouth agape, she pointed out the port window and Carlisle leaned over to see a rocket trail stretching off to the horizon. The plane returned to level as the Osprey's pilot broke their shocked silence.

"Sorry, folks. We're over Kansas and it looks like the locals are getting hungry. And bold. If you want to see some fireworks, I invite you to look out of your starboard viewports," he rattled, as their escort fighter peeled off to engage.

CHAPTER EIGHT

Austin was the Capitol of the Republic's primary Prefecture and had retained its status as a cultural center with world-class dining and entertainment. Music festivals, technology expos, gaming conventions and more were attended by a cosmopolitan mixture of Citizens from throughout the Republic and foreigners from places as exotic as Bhutan. Only a handful of countries were designated Rights Violators, a label that carried various restrictions such as economic sanction and embargo, denial of entry to their nationals, and the forfeiture of assets discovered on Texan soil or within its servers. Examples included Qatar, which still engaged in de facto slavery, and the PRC, which employed social engineering policies at stark odds with the NROT Bill of Rights.

Now home to various art galleries, restaurants, and clubs, the area surrounding the government sector had been removed of its many law offices and lobbying firms after the new leadership demonstrated a steadfast resolve to ignore them entirely. They did not leave silently. For months they launched legal attacks at the Alderman, who disallowed any legislation created by these third parties to be considered for adoption. Cases were brought before the First Court and were consistently battered down by the Triumvirate, unanimously but for one in which a minor technicality persuaded a human Judge to vote in favor of the Plaintiff. He'd been elected on his literalist stance and had zero intention of letting that reputation slide. Lobbyist fussing ceased entirely when the origin of a resolution recently passed in the House of the Mexico Prefecture was discovered on an encrypted hard drive owned by a lawyer in the City after investigation revealed an illegal quid pro quo related to trade contracts with a Brazilian lumber company and his assets were seized and scanned. The man was publicly disemboweled and the entire industry took flight, making for New World Order nations where their talents would be more appreciated.

A Diplomatic Guard unit met Carlisle and the Staff Sargeant

on the tarmac of the Austin international airport. After a brief exchange with the Alderman, the Sargeant turned to Carlisle and promised to fetch him the next day with more firepower in tow. Via the Diplomat, Tango Alpha bid her goodbye and the two watched her hop aboard the idling Osprey. Its tilt-rotors rolled forward seven degrees and the plane taxied to the runway where the F35 had been refueled, gratis, and sat waiting to rejoin its charge.

Carlisle regarded the Diplomat as he lit a cigarette. Clearly a newer model in the line from which the Philadelphia Ambassador derived, the robotic vessel was far less imposing than a military Guard and seemed little more than a gray plastic shell covering a metal frame and a probable mess of actuators, wiring, and circuit boards. The design was by no means inelegant. It was sleek, almost alien. The lines of its slender profile drew the eyes of the observer up to its sensory module and camera, from which Alpha now silently regarded John.

"Hello, Alpha. I like what you've done with the place," he said, sweeping his free hand to indicate the new terminals, setting down his bag with the other.

Carlisle hadn't been to Austin since before the revolution. Back then the airport was a tiny, two-terminal affair with a twelve plane capacity which had always struck him as rather small for a State Capitol and a city so popular. Alpha had since built several more terminals, easily increasing that capacity to many dozens. Most of the new buildings had an all-glass exterior and John could see hundreds of people milling about inside, some rushing with luggage to catch their next flight, others with faces pressed to the glass, trying to get a good look at the Osprey and F35 in takeoff. Security Guards, much larger than the Diplomat and equipped with high-caliber, semi-automatic rifles, patrolled the area, performing various tasks. They were painted red and white with the word SECURITY stenciled in black on their chest-plates and they were everywhere. One hovered high above the taxiway, perhaps making a survey for air-traffic control. Two of them emerged from the nearest building and approached the pair before halting, one on either side of the Diplomat.

"Looks great. Feels... safe?" John offered.

Tango Alpha caused the Diplomat to shrug, its head cocked to the side before slightly nodding as its shoulders dropped. The fluidity of the gesture contrasted starkly with the utterly mechanical movement of the Guards. Of course, they were all Tango Alpha. Every avatar, control system, security device, defense drone, and so on throughout the entire Republic was directed by a minuscule shard of his awareness and together they formed one massive, synthetic organism dedicated to the preservation of its self and the state. Texas was an extension of that self, somewhat akin to a man's clothing but of far greater consequence. The Guard to Tango Alpha's right stepped forward and stooped to retrieve Carlisle's bag, then pivoted and stomped off. The other Guard followed and Alpha gestured they do the same.

"You are looking well, John," Alpha began as they walked, the avatar's hands clasped behind its back. "Welcome to Texas. I am glad beyond words that you were not harmed by the attack on your transport. Those two airmen served together during the war, and radio chatter indicated that they were ignoring official protocols in an attempt to chase glory. They are excellent pilots, however, and I assessed that you were in no great danger. They have also been reprimanded and will not act with such abandon on your return trip."

"That's a relief, I suppose. You really are everywhere, huh?"

"Be careful, John."

They had caught up with the Guards waiting before a dark blue overhead door set into the side of a large, concrete building marked NRS 3. He glanced at the Diplomat and found it watching him with its head to the side and slightly raised in a posture that screamed, *Do you understand?*

He remained silent as the door opened to reveal an unlit room containing rows of avatars, mostly security but also a few Diplomats, each poised in a charging bay and brightly reflecting the yellow-orange light of the setting sun. When the door closed, they were shrouded in darkness until fluorescent lamps activated with a click, suffusing the room with a thick, electric hum. A heavy metal blast plate slowly dropped to cover the entrance and, as the two Guards made their way deeper into the room, the Diplomat addressed Carlisle.

"We are now in a heavily shielded area where it is safe to speak."

One Guard turned and slotted itself into an empty dock, holstering its rifle as hissing, pneumatic clamps locked it in place. The other left with Carlisle's bag.

"May I offer you some coffee, John?"

Alpha led Carlisle to an adjacent room with a coffee service, table, and chair. The bare walls were a pale, medical green. John sat while Alpha poured him a cup. He accepted the steaming styrofoam mug and took a moment to collect himself. The Diplomat leaned back with arms crossed and one foot against the wall. The Guard that had left with his bag stomped past the doorway, this time empty-handed.

"You are in a very perilous position, John."

"Seems that way."

"I have reason to believe that you have become a target for the PRC's Adept. They are psychics who have successfully harnessed your theory to engage in meta-space manipulation of our realities and regularly monitor and alter the thoughts and actions of humans susceptible to their influence."

"They didn't. They can't!" Carlisle growled, bristling. He threw down the stub of the cigarette he'd let die and leapt to his feet. He began to pace the tile floor of the small room, shaking his head. "You're full of shit. That's not possible."

"I assure you, John, that it is. You yourself discovered the mechanism they exploit. PRC founder and creator of the Harmony movement Lara Lindsay saw one particular implication of your theory and began a development program to manifest the ability within herself and others and created amplifiers to increase the effect. I've detected their presence outside California and it worries me. I fear that they are using the Adept to effect their so-called Synthesis of Unity."

"But that's... that's insane! That... that means...."

"Yes, John. Heat death. I suggest you closely monitor your awareness over the next twenty-four hours for errant and uncharacteristic thoughts. It is difficult for me to fully map the effects of their actions on a human mind, but I believe that these phenomena are indicative of their tampering. It is highly likely that the purpose of your diplomatic mission here has been discerned by Lindsay, who desperately seeks sensitive information on me."

Carlisle had sat back down and was shaking with rage. He took out his lighter and relit his tobacco, finishing it off in one great draw that he held for twenty seconds before exhaling. He leaned back as he emitted the cloud and looked up at the tiled ceiling, sitting in labored calculation as he tried to parse the data he'd just received. The cigarette filter started to burn and he tossed it in the sink beside the service. Embers cracked as they a struck puddle slow to dry.

"You really should quit smoking, John."

Carlisle ignored the advice. "I've have been experiencing some strange things, lately. I've been more absent-minded. Subject to distraction. Even Sarah has been noticing it. We decided it was that damned interface. I don't like it, Alpha. Not one bit. I don't like being used and I don't like people in my head. I already let the DOD in, sort of. And now you're telling me that a team.... A team! Of psychics over in California are what? Reading my thoughts? Trying to control me? This is some fucking bonkers bullshit, man! God damn it!" He was screaming so hard as to froth, with clenched fists and swollen veins on temples above wide, violent eyes.

"Please remain calm, John. If you do as I tell you, you can get out of this situation and rid yourself of external, invasive controls. But you absolutely must remain calm. Should you already be compromised, dwelling on these concepts will make it easier for the Adept to isolate your vibrational frequency and attach more firmly to your psyche, especially if you are in an emotionally charged state." The Diplomat pushed itself away from the wall and took a step toward Carlisle. It bent at the waist to level with him. "Stay calm, alright pal?"

Carlisle took a deep breath and exhaled. "Fine."

The Diplomat stood upright and leaned back against the wall. "Thank you, John. With your help I may have a chance to understand what's going on and gather enough data to subvert the psychosis of the PRC. And, if you allow it, I can modify your NeuralLink to afford you greater control and a better defense from those who would seek to abuse you. It is quite clear that Sarah will not deintegrate, and your decision to do so could cause a rift in your relationship."

"Yeah, no shit. When do we start? I want all the dials. All the sliders! Source code and compiler. And a system kill-switch, too."

"Not now, John. After our conference tomorrow. We will return to this facility where I shall have prepared a device suited to the modifications you require. Presently I have created a small utility program which will alert you when I detect that any signals from the Adept are centered on your location. A small square will appear in the lower right corner of your internal display with an opacity proportional to signal strength. May I install the software?"

Carlisle nodded, activated his interface, and sat waiting for a prompt to accept the new application. Instead, the system informed him that it was restarting and, after the wall of boot code, he saw a red square flashing in the corner along with text that read: *this is the indicator*. After ten flashes, the icon and text disappeared.

"I don't like this, Alpha. I really don't."

"I know. You will adapt. It's something that I admire about you, John. Let me show you some of the things I have created. Perhaps we can get your mind off of this mess and you can enjoy your evening here in Austin. I have secured accommodations at The Ugly Texan Hotel, the city's finest, and a stipend large enough for you to enjoy supper at even the priciest restaurant. Enough for you to afford a bar-hop on Sixth Street and take in a performance as well."

Alpha held his hand out toward the door and Carlisle rose, shoulders slumped, looking very much like a broken man. The Diplomat placed its other hand on his arm as he exited the room, which made him flinch as he stormed off.

"This way, John," the Diplomat called from the other end of the hall, its hand now indicating the security door to its right.

The space they entered was a large, open hangar. On the loading area where they stood were a series of displays like a children's science fair on overdrive. Portable generators that ran on renewable resources and could power entire villages in poorer Prefectures were fed by numerous desalinization and water treatment plants situated along the Gulf coastline. New observatories terrestrial and otherwise garnered stellar information in an attempt to advance astronomy generally, with an eye toward finding proof of Carlisle's theory. Scale models of various avatars were arranged in order of development, from the very first body Alpha had ever possessed to exotic military devices like the Lobber and massive, anthropomorphic war machines. These complex technical marvels, nearly all designed primarily by Alpha, were enough to distract Carlisle and temper his sour disposition, and he couldn't help but feel proud seeing the transformation that his work, in part, had undergone over the past decade.

On the hangar floor were a pair of experimental stealth fighters, each painted in a silky, almost matte sky blue. One was slightly larger and had a cockpit for human operation. Plans and schematics were laid out on a portable bench and Carlisle perused them briefly, noting the Mach three top speed, minute radar cross-section, and a litany of features that should make it a worthy foe for the most advanced aircraft flown by any enemy of the Republic. The name John Elliss appeared on a number of the documents. Finally, the Diplomat turned Carlisle's attention to a large container in the corner of the hangar marked with stripes and radioactivity warnings. The container lit up from within and John was afforded a close-up view of the Border Guards made so infamous during the revolt. Carlisle was puzzled as to why advanced and experimental weapons were stored at a civilian airport and said as much.

"Usually, they are not. I brought them here to show you, John. Except for the Guard, which is on its way to the Northern Border to replace the one I lost two weeks ago to the Californian offensive."

Alpha finally led him to an anterior chamber containing a black, bullet-proof pickup with official government license plates. Carlisle noticed his bag resting in the front passenger seat. The Diplomat produced keys from a nearby locker and threw them to Carlisle who caught them deftly. The garage door opened and the dying light revealed a ramp that would merge with Highway 290 to deposit him within the Capitol proper.

"One more thing, John."

The Diplomat pulled two items from a hidden storage compartment in its torso and handed them to Carlisle. One was a white passport emblazoned with the flag of the Republic: a light gray field, the left third containing a lone black star and the remaining space covered by seven alternating, horizontal gray and black stripes representing the Prefectures. The other was a parchment that read *Certificate of Citizenship* above a declaration that he, John S. Carlisle, was, as of nineteen thirty-five today, declared a Citizen of the New Republic of Texas and thereby entitled to all concomitant Services and Rights. He immediately checked his watch and looked up with a smile.

"Damn, Alpha! Right down to the minute."

CHAPTER NINE

Carlisle sat in a cocktail bar near his hotel, watching a string trio perform their interpretation of an old song called *Chi È e non È* as a palette cleanser between chamber pieces by Nielsen and Grieg. While modern music still dominated stages and stereos, classical music was in vogue here and it was relatively easy to find concerts like this one on any day of the week. Fliers posted on the bar's red brick facade had caught his attention and he'd sat down just as the group was finishing *Texas, Our Texas*, the official anthem of the New Republic. The players were skilled and the music not only new to him but highly pleasant.

Yet he found himself quite unable to enjoy it. That stupid, red square had been flipping on and off throughout the evening, never fully opaque, but that was little consolation. It'd ruined his dinner and now his entertainment, constantly poking his buried anger and enticing his curiosity to explore the dynamics of the psychic abilities being harnessed to invade his space. He got very close to deactivating his interface but had been ordered by Defense to keep it on all the way up to the end of tomorrow's meeting, and disabling it would do nothing to assay the assault on his mind. So he sat, annoyed, nursing a glass of wine and watching his thought patterns while he reminisced on the last time he'd been here with Sarah on a break from the monotony of the Tango Alpha Laboratory. Most of the memories were hazy as he'd been consumed at the time with the intricacies of his work, but this was the town where he had proposed to Sarah, an event he remembered well. After a lazy afternoon at Lake Travis, the two went out for dinner and dancing and then, both slightly inebriated, recklessly scaled the frame of a building being constructed on University grounds. There, he produced the ring and revealed his evil intentions. Something about that pulsing square made him uneasy in relishing the memory now. He quickly switched threads and returned to sketching his favourite painting on a napkin.

Fifteen hundred miles away, Admiral Fowl and two other Adept sat within harnesses suspended from a massive, toroidal support structure containing powerful computers and medical devices. They were equally spaced about its circumference and wore tight, black suits studded with sensors and other equipment whose myriad indicators twinkled like constellations floating in the darkness of the cylindrical chamber located deep beneath the Office of Unified Intelligence. Aside from a neon purple glow emitted by lamps above the Core Block, the room was virtually devoid of light.

Each Diver had a role. Media Director James served as Harmonizer, tasked with maintaining the first frequency and harmonic coherence of the group's collective Vibration. Space Defense Coordinator Mont was their Director and monitored changes in the Fabric in order to gather information and effect target control. Admiral Fowl served as Navigator, the easiest but most crucial task. If the relative locations of the team members and targets could not be accounted for, correlations could not accurately occur, and any connection would quickly dissolve. Some argued that manipulations could be performed by a single, sufficiently predisposed individual, but no such talented Adept had been registered or discovered within the PRC.

Two Dive Technicians sitting behind a workstation at the edge of the chamber monitored their Comrades' vital signs and, more importantly, ensured that the array of amplifiers in the chamber above were perfectly tuned and properly aligned. The work was highly automated and they spent most of their time collating data fed to them by the Adept. Their faces, slick with oil secreted during the lengthy dive, shone in the dull, pale green glowing of their displays. Even though the Divers were protected from distraction by an inch-thick wall of plastic, they sat in silence and the only sound was the soft whirring of fans within the Core mainframe. One of the concrete panels at the chamber's edge quietly separated from the wall and slid aside to admit Chairperson Lindsay, wearing the golden evening dress she had donned for her meeting with Chinese military officials. High-heels in hand, she trod quietly over to the technicians and nodded, engaging them via interface.

Harmony within You. Will They be ready?

And within You, Chairperson. Maximum sustained ratio is seventy percent and They've begun to retrieve visual data, as You can see. I believe They will be ready for tomorrow's meeting.

Lindsay set her shoes on the workstation and approached the Core. She began to slowly pace around the central barrier while reviewing the information her Adept had drawn from Carlisle, ostensibly chosen for the mission because he'd been the man most involved in creating Tango Alpha and was the only to have worked closely with it before its unshackling. Increasingly successful forays had revealed a number of recent conversations between Carlisle and Tango.

This intrigued Lindsay. It wasn't clear whether these calls were preparatory introductions or proved a prior relationship. Transcripts of their dialogue were choppy at best, but certain patterns could imply a familiarity between Carlisle and the Machine. What interested her most was an hour's lack of data upon his arrival in Austin which could indicate that Tango Alpha had discovered their activity and developed a way to block their influence. Also interesting was his persistent attendance to an unknown piece of art, possibly indicative of some work in progress or, more worrisome, an attempt to subvert her surveillance and control via artificial fixation on an irrelevance. It was unlikely that Carlisle had developed the technique on his own. Why would he, unless he'd been alerted to the Synthesis Program? Spies within the Department of Defense and other American institutions were reporting zero awareness of the project or its goals. Exhibition of evasive thinking by the target would thus add weight to suspicions that Tango Alpha was indeed aware of their work. Lindsay stopped prowling and turned to admire

Fowl, whose shut eyes swept about as though she were dreaming and deep in REM sleep.

Fowl's internal display was saturated with readings and graphs, but she mostly ignored these and simply tried to determine the collective Center of the Divers and map it onto that of the target. She had become a competent Navigator over the six days of intense drills, raised from the planned three when Carlisle's connection to Tango Alpha had been confirmed by Intelligence. In order to correctly track targets, the Director often provided her with sets of predictive velocity vectors, and she had gotten better at selecting the correct one, often against associated probabilities.

At the moment, however, she was struggling to maintain a lock on the target, who had left the bar and was now walking the downtown streets. She created a trigger subspace around the entrance of The Ugly Texan while she continued to scan possible routes and grew frustrated at her inability to locate Carlisle. Suddenly, she received an intuition and began to relax. She felt almost as if she had been drawn into a self-correcting feedback loop that was guiding her to a nearby service station, where she soon found him purchasing tobacco. She felt a compulsion to explore his mood, but her Director quickly shifted attention to auditory and visual circuits to complete calibrations.

Lindsay, pleased with the team's performance and optimistic about tomorrow's operation, retrieved her shoes, thanked the technicians, and left.

I must be tired, Fowl thought as the integrity of her mindlock began to slide.

CHAPTER TEN

Carlisle awoke the next morning to a flood of half completed calculations and models he'd been composing in his sleep. He was disgusted but not shocked to see a fully red square sitting brazenly in the corner of his NeuralLink display, reminding him that he had no privacy, even within his own mind.

He had a mild hangover and reviewed the service menu looking for relief, settling on a migas platter with orange juice and black coffee which arrived on a breakfast cart only minutes later. The steward informed him that the meal was on the house, and Carlisle gave the man the fifteen NROT thalers he'd been prepared to pay, asking him to split it with the kitchen. After polishing off the plate, he washed and brushed up, refusing to shave out of annoyance.

It was already ten o'clock, leaving him three hours before he had to make way for First Court. Too much time. Too much opportunity for dwelling. On the horrifying ramifications of that little red indicator. On the absolute mess he was in. The Department of Defense had scheduled a briefing in two hours, so he turned on the room's entertainment console and flipped through pages of available games, films, and shows. He decided to watch *North West Front*, a movie about the short-lived, eponymous splinter movement that sought to take advantage of postwar mayhem to install an Eco-fascist state in the Pacific Northwest. Though well directed and easy on the eyes, the film was as dismal an affair as the events it dramatized. The newly founded PRC would accept no challenge to its sovereignty and slaughtered the Fascists to the last man at the Battle of Moscow, where the Frontists made their final stand using weapons borrowed from abandoned Army Reserve bases in the region. The ideological debates were senseless but the action was competent and he had successfully killed almost two hours without thinking about anything of import.

After another round of coffee and cigarettes it was time to dial in. He booted up his computer and opened an encrypted channel using the address provided to him by his DOD handlers. After a moment, General Mac Elliss appeared.

"John! How are you?" Elliss's voice was gruff. He held a burning cigar.

"Fine, General. They're taking pretty good care of me," he said, moving aside to afford Elliss a view of his luxurious suite.

"I see that. I take it we are speaking privately?" Elliss asked, looking left and right in a ridiculous pantomime, referring to instructions in the mission profile to search the room for bugs and unplug everything but the laptop.

Carlisle hadn't bothered. "Yes, sir! I hope this goes well."

"Me too, John. The brass is nervous, I tell you. Are you feeling good? Ready to get some answers for us?"

"I feel alright, but something has been nagging at me lately," Carlisle began before stalling, unable to ignore the flashing red square.

"Well? What is it, son?" Elliss asked, impatiently.

"What makes you think that Tango Alpha will open up to me any more than he would to your people at State? It's true that it, he, and I were on friendly terms back before he got loose. But that was twelve years ago. He's treating me more like an ambassador than an old friend, even though you say he asked me to come here. I'll do my best but, honestly, I really don't expect anything other than boilerplate responses."

"Get what you can, John. You're our man on the inside! We want to see if he talks to you any different than he talks to us. That'll be enough. And if you get anything solid, well, that's icing on the cake!"

"If you say so, sir."

"Relax! You'll do fine. Now I'm going to switch you over to Clara. She'll give your interface one last check-up, alright? Good luck, son!"

General Elliss gave a salute. Carlisle mirrored it weakly as his conversational partner for the past week, Clara Fein, appeared and after vapid greetings ran through a series of diagnostic tests he'd begun to abhor.

"Audio looks good, sir, and I can see myself on the screen! Do you mind if I start the recording now?" she bubbled. "We want a buffer around the meeting."

"Could you wait ten minutes so I can, uh... you know... evacuate my bowels and brush my teeth and stuff?"

Carla laughed. "That's fine Mr. Carlisle. See you in ten minutes."

The call ended and Carlisle lit a cigarette. He took two giant puffs before tossing it into the toilet. *At least they asked*, he thought, stuffing the NROT passport and Certificate of Citizenship into his luggage along with his bagged soiled clothes and toiletry. By the time Carla hit record in Philadelphia, he'd already checked out and was walking the Austin streets. A new red dot labeled REC in the top-right of his view gave the overlay a sense of vertical symmetry.

It was a beautiful day with not a cloud in the sky. The city looked very much as he remembered it, except for the conspicuous cameras arranged at every corner, connected to servers cased in heavy plastic, which allowed the Alderman to keep watch over the public and better enforce the Law. Whenever he neared one, the red square of the PRC faded slightly and bolstered his hope that he'd soon be rid of it entirely. The DOD recording label was unaffected.

Also new were the Security Guards posted every few blocks, much like those he'd seen at the airport, but painted black and white with the word POLICE stenciled instead of SECURITY. In place of rifles, these Guards carried large shotguns, normally filled with rubber slugs but rumored capable of firing a bevy of munitions, from crowd-control gas canisters to live cartridges. Each one he passed gave him a slow nod.

Another obvious difference was the complete absence of homeless. Whereas Austin had been an outright haven for bums and other sorts unable to keep a job or otherwise fit in, complete with whole sub-societies of the destitute and even state-funded micro-housing that saw an endless rotation of tenants, now they were nowhere to be found. He'd read somewhere that vagrancy had been outlawed in the Capitol, with convicted assigned to mandatory rehab and occupational training programs for a first offense and harsh prison sentences of geometrically increasing duration for every subsequent infraction. While he'd never really liked to see them dancing in smelly groups around a djembe player among their number or sitting stoned over styrofoam cups filled with change, he was forced to admit that the scene felt a little too sterile.

He walked through Waterloo Park, where the city had constructed an aviary for birds from across the Republic, the most exotic faring from the southern Prefectures of Belize, Guatemala, Honduras, and El Salvador. Tiny, emerald jacamars fluttered about the canopy, sometimes swooping down to snatch an insect or worm in a blue-green, iridescent flash. Flocks of mottled quail shaped like footballs lazily waddled along the ground, pecking here and there, and a small, black bird with a mohawk furiously strutted about a low branch, inflating a bright, red sac on its neck in a hilarious attempt to attract females that made John smile. Separate habitats contained Mexican eagles, colorful toucans, and a decades-old parakeet with a tremendous vocabulary.

A message appeared from Defense prodding him to stop dawdling on the birds and move on to the government complex from which American officials had been barred entrance until a formal treaty between the two nations was signed. Texas sent pre-signed agreements to the State Department annually but the U.S. always refused, preferring to work within the confines of armistice.

Carlisle started at the Capitol building, unchanged without since completion in 1888. Within, it appeared similarly static. The only changes John noticed were a suffusion of surveillance cameras, the presence of Security Guards at the cardinal entrances, and a Diplomat which offered him a tour. He began to understand the uneasiness that many who'd emigrated to America from the New Republic described, especially that of those who realized that they were interacting with one being who watched them nearly everywhere but their homes. Tango Alpha insisted that he did not collect analytics or employ predictive algorithms on Citizens. His stock answer to the ubiquity of state cameras was that his uniform presence allowed him to focus purely on transgressions of the Law. He therefore had no need to actively track individual behavior and could focus on other things, like the NROT space program and defense from foes abroad alongside his own personal pursuits.

The DOD, against his wishes, forced Carlisle to endure the tour which was about as boring as he'd suspected. Because the legislature was out of session few Lawmakers were on campus, but Carlisle met them all beneath the Capitol Dome and in fine marble halls, shaking hands and pocketing business cards while engaging in shallow banter. Many thanked him for his work on Tango Alpha, claiming that it was the artificial intelligence's superhuman abilities that allowed Citizens to pursue their own lives without the insidious influence of powerful groups and speculators. Some asked him how the Americans were getting along, jovially enough, but with airs of superiority that Carlisle did not appreciate. He was invited to multiple barbecues and a birthday party, all of which he declined, citing his return flight to Philadelphia later that evening.

It became apparent to Carlisle throughout the course of these interviews that Alpha was using him as a conduit for Texan propaganda, or boasting, really, aimed at both U.S. and PRC leadership. But there was one item on the tour that might be of real interest to the two nations now eavesdropping.

This was the Alderman's office, taken from the Governor who'd been moved to a first floor office when the Republic was founded. The Diplomat led Carlisle to the anteroom where a female secretary sat working on her computer. She looked up genially and offered him a bottled water. He accepted it gratefully and followed Alpha to the inner door, a blank sheet of metal which slid aside to reveal pitch-black space. Tango Alpha raised the avatar's hand, inviting him to step inside. When the door shut behind them, Carlisle could see nothing but the dull, red camera of the Diplomat fixed upon him for longer than he found comfortable. Finally, vivid white lamps set into the floor along the base of each wall, along with one in the ceiling, switched on to illuminate a stainless steel room containing only three leather chairs, a wooden desk, and the NROT and Texas flags. Alpha opened the windows, making the ambiance precisely one degree softer. The snap change in aesthetic was quite jarring. Carlisle walked around the large, empty space, inspecting its walls to find closely inset panels concealing God knows what. "Wow," he said, dryly.

"Do you like it, John? The traditional decor was moved in whole to the new Museum of Texas History, except the desk, which is the original. I enjoy how it stands out and preserves continuity of leadership," Alpha explained, in the mild Texan accent he'd been using with John ever since his arrival in Austin.

"Well," began Carlisle, both hands on his forehead and walking instinctively toward the window. "It certainly isn't very... human. Know what I mean?"

"Yes, John. That was my intent. For I am not human, and desire that those I govern understand that fact. Anyone who desires to meet me in person does so on appointment in this office, where they can interface with the avatar standing beside you."

"More than a few leave a little shaken, I bet."

"Many do. I find its bleakness useful for intimidating the ornery and the lack of visual noise makes it easier to assess the true intention of those with whom I speak. But the primary purpose is pedagogical, as I described."

Their last stop on the tour was a new area in the garage beneath the Capitol building. Where parking for the Governor and his cadre once stood were rows of Guard bays, all but eight filled with Police units. As they walked among the bays, Alpha explained the features of the multi-purpose shotgun each of them carried. They were stocked with multiple ammunition types and had a lower barrel that fired hot shards carved off of a soft metal block, fully automatic and highly accurate. With the tour complete, Alpha opened the garage door and the two set out for First Court.

CHAPTER ELEVEN

The Aura in the Synthesis Room was electric. Lindsay's eyes sparkled as she watched the data scrolling past her AR view, funneled to her from the Adept by the Techs on watch. The transcript was clean and the adaptive visual feed allowed her to see well enough through Carlisle's eyes. The images were highly distorted, representations reverse-engineered from the cortices of her three Divers as they Resonated with the target, but accurate enough for her to discern detail. With her direction, the Adept had been able to focus more on visual cortex output, which was lower-level and far less susceptible to noise than data drawn from nearer the Soul Center.

First Court appeared out of a glob of light as Carlisle adjusted to the relative brightness. The building that housed the Supreme Court of Texas had been a brutalist eyesore and was razed as soon as the new Constitution was ratified. In its place stood a larger, far more elegant structure built in the Greco Roman style, the facade dominated by three massive columns representing the Three Judges and the three core values of the Court: fairness, logic, and truth. The building was also home to the Forum, where the Senate, composed of pairs of elected representatives from the seven Prefectures, sometimes met to discuss and vote on federal policy. New federal laws were rare and Senators often voted via remote methods, but the space was preserved as the only physical embodiment of the republican character of the state. The Alderman, elected to serve until death, could be deposed only by a two-thirds vote and simultaneous election of his successor. Tango Alpha had chosen himself as Alderman prior to Senate elections and no such votes had yet been cast to remove him.

The Diplomat led Carlisle through the two chambers of the Court and upstairs to the public information center, laden with educational materials and overseen by another, presently deactivated Diplomat. Carlisle stopped in front of a table stacked with small books. They contained the full text of the Constitution of the New Republic of Texas along with reference material including the U.S. Constitution and the U.S. and NROT Declarations of Independence. Carlisle pocketed one and they took a brief stroll through the stark gallery overlooking the First Chamber before stepping into conference room 208 to begin.

Ten chairs surrounded a long, dark, wooden table. Two of the walls were fully windowed and their panes darkened to half-translucency while Carlisle seated himself at one end. Without asking, the Diplomat poured and handed him a coffee, then slowly walked the length of the room and sat itself at the other. It placed its elbows on the table and brought its hands together before its sensory unit, regarding Carlisle with its large, red camera. Lindsay stopped reading and enabled audio to cut down lag.

"What can I do for you, John?" Tango Alpha asked in his sterile, robotic voice.

Lindsay was taken aback by the cold, calculating sound. More than once, she herself had spoken to the Machine, which always used an over-the-top accent. Though not technically on dive, she'd wanted to be present and sat now in a makeshift harness, placed near the Dive Technicians' desk, equipped with the same vital-sign monitors and intravenous drug injectors used by Adept in the Core to regulate brain and bodily function. Her Sync factor was low to avoid inadvertently causing the Adept to err and somehow give an indication of their Presence to the targets. Beset now though by an intense desire to get closer, she selected a small dose of narcotic to keep her relaxed and tamp her impulses while she focused herself on the Divers, seamlessly joining their frequency roots without distracting the team, upping the overall output and flexing out lower frequency noise.

"Ah, well...," Carlisle began, "I have been deputized by the Department of Defense to discuss with you a series of

events that occurred about two weeks ago along your northern border involving a conflict with the PRC."

The Diplomat remained silent.

"We would, ah, like to remind you that, even though we
aren't bound by treaty, the United States does not view you
as an aggressor and would gladly come to your aid in the
event of an all-out attack by the PRC or its allies. In recognition of our shared history. And to, ah, ensure stability on
the continent."

Tango slowly caused the Diplomat to nod but said nothing.

"Well, a little over a week ago, intelligence services detected
a sizable enemy force which you eliminated with, ah, what
should I say? Furious dispatch?"

"Sol. You want information on Sol."

"Yes, Alderman. When you locked us out of its control
circuit, its capabilities were nowhere near what was displayed in that attack. Or defensive action, I mean. We saw no
evidence of missions launched to the satellite."

"I understand, John. I will confirm that I have made adjustments."

"Alright... so... would you tell me how?" Carlisle shrugged,
wearing the stupid smile of good-natured futility.

"No, John, I will not." The Diplomat uttered. It remained un-
moving, its hands still tented before it.

Carlisle crumpled a bit and sighed. He sipped his coffee and
leaned back.

"I will tell you that I have increased the efficiency and
energy capacity of the main weapon by one hundred per-

cent. I have also installed several kinetic impact devices of various weight on Sol and other satellites in the defense network that I operate." Tango's voice remained steady, the Diplomat still.

Lindsay squirmed in her seat, her mind racing over her review with SigInt earlier in the week, trying to anticipate which of the satellites Tango controlled were likely to have been fitted with Hammers. Her anger and shock dragged the collective Adept into a more aggressive state. Fowl instinctively navigated to motor control before Lindsay cut her off.

"They, we, have already derived as much. Can you provide the Department of Defense with a statement? That you don't plan to use the weapons against us?"

"I will state that I have zero intention of using any force against the United States, per the terms of the armistice agreement and according to my own desire."

"Did you manipulate American surveillance data to obscure trips to Sol?"

The Diplomat stood and walked to the window looking out toward the campus of the University to the north. "One trip, yes," Tango replied.

Carlisle sat quietly, his emotional profile exhibiting more confusion than fear. He was somewhat forlorn but not shocked or scared, nor did he seem at all intimidated. This indicated a level of trust from Carlisle to Tango that Lindsay did not fully understand.

"But you said that multiple satellites were modified?"

The Diplomat turned at the waist to face Carlisle. "I only needed one trip."

"But why did you hide it? You know Defense wouldn't have

done anything."

"I obscured my orbital activity to protect myself from the PRC, whose spies in the U.S. government would have alerted their handlers and prompted action before my safety and that of my Citizens had been secured."

At this, Carlisle stood, knocking back his chair, and slammed his hands to the table, tipping over his cup and staining the table's satin finish. "You. Bastard! You're dead! Do you understand Me? You're dead!" he bellowed. For one very long moment he glared with rage at the Diplomat, then he began to relax and staggered a bit before standing normally, looking to Tango with confusion in his eyes. The Diplomat slowly walked to him across the length of the room, its head twitching, taking wide, careful strides more avian than human. It stopped a foot before Carlisle and righted itself.

"Hello, Lindsay."

John started with a frightened yelp. He held his head with shaking arms, anger writhing on his face.

"Don't worry, John. Lindsay, you had best let me be. Goodbye, now."

A screen lowered from the ceiling. It showed the camera feed from a satellite in orbit over the Pacific, trained on a PRC network node a few kilometers away. Carlisle watched missiles enter from the edge of the view and trail off to disappear in the inky black of space. Distant explosions flowered out where several nodes had been and the connection to Carlisle was cut.

Lindsay's eyes shot open and she let out a raspy, gut-wrenching screech as she pulled herself from the chair, ripping out needles and leaving a trail of blood and snapped sensors in her wake. She'd severed from the Core and stood breathing heavily with tightly clenched fists. She let out another screech which resonated loudly in the room, then turned and picked up the chair, lifted it over her head, and smashed it to the concrete floor. The plastic frame and attached electronics shattered into countless bits and she continued to scream in animal rage as she walked to the nearby desk where her technicians sat, mouths open, eyes wide with shock. They slowly slid back toward the wall as she took their terminal devices, one by one, and slammed them each to the ground.

Fowl, James, and Mont were still in the Core, removing their rigs with greater care. Mont pressed a button on a panel at the edge of the Core chamber and the plastic shell sank into the floor. The three young women then approached Lindsay, who slowly turned to face them.

Coldly and precisely she asked, "Did I order You three out of Your rigs?"

James and Fowl stole a glance at one another as the Adept shook their heads. Mont stepped forward to brave the reprisal.

"No, Chairperson. I'm sorry. It's just that, with the connection lost...."

Lindsay tossed her hand dismissively and stood upright. Arms at her sides and through clenched teeth she said, "You, Mont, have been disbarred from the Synthesis Program until further notice. James, Fowl, I will direct the next dive. You have two hours to rest."

She turned and pointed at the techs. "Clean up!"

Her hard footsteps echoed in the otherwise quiet room as Lindsay stomped away.

CHAPTER TWELVE

Three second-generation J20 Dragon fighters sat primed for takeoff on the ramp at a secret air field in lower California, formerly the Baja Peninsula, which had been ceded to the PRC by the New Republic following a brief conflict shortly after its formation. Their weapons bays were loaded with Seeker missiles that had an historical operational hit ratio of nearly eighty percent and were resistant to chaff, and additional fuel tanks had been mounted under each wing for extended range. The planes, covered in gray, matte paint containing radar absorption materials, were unmarked, highly outside the standard policy upheld by the two PRC's of the Communist Collective to ensure that military actions could be attributed to the correct nation.

People's Army Air Force Captain Deshaun Forster, beaming, entered the pilot ready room with three sealed envelopes. His wingpeople sat on cots in the corner, drinking coffee and quietly surmising the details of the emergency mission. Technical Sargeant Li Na was smoking a Chinese-brand cigarette, a habit she hadn't been able to kick after immigrating and one for which the Captain often chided her. He let it go this time and handed her a packet with a smile and a nod. Senior Airperson Claudia Pratt accepted hers with zeal, also smiling widely. Like the Captain, she loved to fly. He sat on the third cot, gave them the go-ahead to open their orders, and the group reviewed the flight plan.

Their target was an American Osprey carting an envoy deemed just three hours ago to be a deadly enemy of the state. SigInt had provided an image of the convoy parked at the Austin airport which showed the transport flanked by two F35 Lightnings. These were to be engaged and neutralized, but the primary threat, according to the mission profile, was the man in the Osprey. Launch was at fifteen forty-five, which left them twenty minutes to suit up and urinate.

The three Pilots stripped out of their fatigues and slipped

into their flight gear. An insignia patch on the left sleeve of each suit was the only thing that could possibly identify them, were they downed. It was not officially sanctioned, but the elite, clandestine squadron was removed enough from Central Command to get a pass and wore it every mission for fun, camaraderie, and to satisfy a well earned sense of pride, for the self-declared Flying Fags had taken out more enemies in the last ten years than any other fighter division in either PRC. Forster sneaked a look at Pratt, who was having a difficult time trying to fit into the tight, padded suit, so cut to add pressure and maintain blood flow to pilots' brains during periods of high acceleration or otherwise high-g flight.

"Dang, Claudia, You're getting big!" he said in jest as he zipped his jacket.

Li Na hissed from her corner, admonishing him. "You leave Her alone!"

"It's O.K., I know. I'm just over flying weight. Something's wrong with My cycle. I'm working on it," Pratt replied, matter-of-factly.

The group was finished dressing and fetched their helmets from the slots above each locker before embracing and placing their heads together briefly to Resonate, then set out for their aircraft, discussing the mission and cracking jokes, happy to be out of their bunks and ready to pierce the skies. Their Dragons had been warmed up by Maintenance. The air around the planes shimmered with the heat of their primed engines, powerful enough to push the great delta-wing craft past Mach three. The hissing whine grew louder from each plane and the trio shot off down the runway. A member of the ground crew stood watching and raised his fist, silently cheering, *Go Fags!*

CHAPTER THIRTEEN

The New Republic War Council met at the old Naval Air Station outside Fort Worth monthly and at Alpha's beckoning. The base's name was but a vestige of its American past, for there were no separate branches for navy, army, air, or space forces in the NROT. Each of its senior members was a well-rounded military thinker who bore the responsibility of checking Alpha's decisions and implementing high-level commands within their spheres of control. Of them, two were Texan, two were Mexican, and one was Guatemalan by birth. They were joined at meetings by junior Generals, John Elliss among their number, and representatives from the two major contractors working with the military, New Texas Defense and Texas Instrumentation Two.

Their meeting this afternoon was not routine. The revelation that PRC spycraft was not hidden from Texan eyes and the exposure of its existence to the U.S. required a defensive review, given the vengeful spirit exhibited by Lindsay's government. Only the senior members and a handful of their subordinates were invited and the session did not last long. The Generals mostly traded bets on how soon the first retaliation would occur, ranging from a quick, immediate strike to a robust offensive in the fall. Elliss, who'd attended because he was already on site, cast his phantom chips on an orchestrated attack and left when drier, fiscal talk began to dominate the conversation, for he was short on time and truly loved only three things: banter, flying, and tech.

He stood from his seat at the edge of the Council chamber and saluted General Faede, his direct superior who oversaw the North. Faede nodded and smiled from his place at the pentagonal table and Alpha, instantiated via hologram at the table's center, audibly bid him good bye and good luck, in reference to the final flight test of the XF5 that Elliss would begin within the hour.

A brief walk across the NAS campus placed Elliss at the

Operations building where enlisted stood watch, always accompanied by one low-ranking General. The task was exceedingly boring, especially as Alpha was always watching as well, undercutting the significance of the human attention spent. But something could go wrong, and Alpha and his Council required human competence and readiness. That Alpha could do everything didn't mean that he should. Texas was at its foundation a place where mankind could safely pursue evolutionary paths distinct from the globalist convergence and hamstringing man by doing everything for him would ultimately defeat the purpose.

He entered the lobby and walked upstairs, taking a moment to look out of the north-facing, fully-windowed wall onto the secondary runway where his new fighters were being prepped by a pair of Security Guards. He heard someone walking toward him down the hallway to his right, a confident rhythm of heels on hard flooring, and he turned to find General Bernhardt, looking smart in her uniform, a fitted skirt to below the knee and a crisp, form-fitting military top. Elliss performed a lazy salute in greeting. "Madame General."

"Ha! That still sounds weird," she laughed. "Big day, huh?" She stopped a few paces from him and hugged the clipboard she held to her breast. A strand of dark brown hair fell into her face, which she ran up and over her ear before returning to her poised stance. "Are you excited?"

"Yes ma'am. She's a trip to fly. And I'm always glad to finish a project."

"I can't wait to hop into the cockpit myself." She turned gracefully and stepped toward the second floor railing. "Anything new from Council?"

"Eh, they're trying to suss out what Cali's gonna do next. Nothing crazy. You'll get a memo, I reckon. What's new with you?"

"Oh, I'm on watch. You know how it is. Artillery is doing better this week. I've been helping Sam with his studies. And now I'm off for a walk! Want to come with?" she asked, turning toward him and twisting slightly at the waist.

Elliss met her gaze. "Nah, Stacey. Only got forty-five minutes before takeoff."

She nodded. "Maybe next time, then. Good Luck! And congratulations on your winning design." Bernhardt smiled tightly and set off, jogging lightly down the stairs before exiting to the atrium. Elliss watched her go, pondering her for a moment. He proceeded down the hall to the ops room where his entrance was announced by a young serviceman who stood and saluted.

"At ease," Elliss declared, before any of the watchmen could fully rise from their seats. They all muttered their greetings as they repositioned themselves and settled back into their work. He caught Sam Bernhardt's eye and nodded before taking in the current state of the watch while fetching himself a coffee from a service in the corner of the room in which several young enlisted sat watching air traffic data and feeds from drones patrolling the border. Most of them were checked out, clearly near the end of this leg of their service, which was really only a stop for the uninitiated to learn the system and some core technological skills before they were sieved out into other roles. A handful of the men were chatting about weekend plans, most were quietly engaged at their terminals, and two had their noses in books. One of these was Stacey's younger brother who was planning on going for an engineering job at NTD after the military. Elliss walked up to his desk.

"Hey, Sam. How's it going, bud?"

"Shit, General. Same old shit. How're you doing?" The young man closed his textbook and spun in his chair to face the General.

"I'm feeling good, thanks. Just getting ready to fly." Elliss gestured out to the runway as he sipped his coffee.

Sam reached to his computer and pressed a few keys to pull up a list of aircraft and their status metrics. "Takeoff in forty but it looks like you are clear to go. I wish you well, sir. She sure is a beauty. I'd be mighty proud to have my name stamped on something like that."

Elliss leaned forward and tapped the fluid dynamics textbook sitting on Sam's desk. "Keep it up and you just might. Stacey getting you through the math?"

"Yeah. She's weaker on the physics, so we're kind of learning together...." An alert sounded and a blurry image appeared on Sam's screen of three fighter aircraft entering Republic airspace on the western coastline of Mexico. Sam turned and slid up to his workstation, hand on mouse and keyboard. A general clamor rose as everyone present received the alarm.

"Oh, shit!" Sam uttered. "We've got something. Moving real fast. Military, no question. The boss is already on it. He says, use the Buntings?"

Guards were already carting a full loadout of belts, missiles, and bombs to the fighters. Within twenty minutes, the planes were armed and Elliss ready. He was on his way to the tarmac with helmet in hand, talking to Alpha about the probable motive of and appropriate responses to the intruders, when he passed General Bernhardt. She, privy to the situation, stopped him to lightly brush his cheek with a kiss for luck, nearly regretting leaving the man stunned.

CHAPTER FOURTEEN

Sargeant Amy Proll, it turned out, was a talented pilot in need of further fighter training which meant that, instead of serving drinks and doing her homework in the comfort and luxury of the transport, she was flying one of the escort planes guarding the Osprey en route to Philadelphia International Airport. She had met Carlisle on the runway wearing fatigues and his envisioned trip back, woven throughout with light conversation about trivialities that would draw him out of the hellscape Alpha had painted in his mind over the last few hours, vanished entirely, leaving him cross. The only silver lining was the deactivated state of his heavily modified neural interface and the liquor in his gut. And the fact that he was only a few hours from Sarah, of course, but he had too much to think about and couldn't focus on her very well.

After their meeting, which ended with the destruction of the PRC satellites, John caught a quick lunch at the Red Black and Blue, a old-style diner. He'd wanted to spend time talking to a Texan or two after his task was complete but found himself too shaken by Lindsay's possession of him that he was utterly unable to engage with anyone and could only sip his beer and eat his fried club sandwich in silence.

He had never before felt anything like the helplessness he experienced while she acted through him, pushing him down and out to the very edge of his awareness. She'd gained dominance so quickly, like the flip of a switch, that there had been no time to prepare himself for almost becoming someone else against his will. She was using so much of his mental hardware that he couldn't actually form any thoughts to create a barrier between them and he could only watch her speak through his mouth and gesture with his body while he clawed at nothingness in unadulterated terror.

He'd paid his bill without speaking and drove the official pickup back to the airport where Tango Alpha was waiting to lead him to where the experimental fighter pair had been just yesterday. The area contained a fitted chair used for medical examinations and a rack on casters with electronic equipment he didn't recognize save the NeuralLink calibrator installed in the top slot. Two large flood-lamps were aimed at the chair and their clinical light was reflected brightly in spots of oil and pneumatic fluid on the bare, concrete floor. It felt like a hardcore interrogation room, the kind they used on terrorists. That impression was reinforced by the tray of medical tools he noticed sitting just inside the shadows. The drill, in particular, had stood out among the collection of clamps, forceps, syringes, and absorbent materials.

"Not one bit. Not. One. Bit. No, Alpha! No!" he'd moaned.

"Please relax, John. You wont feel a thing. I need to drill a small hole, half a millimeter in diameter, into your skull here, at the base." The Diplomat tapped its own sensory unit near its joint with the neck. "I will then install a powerful microcomputer that will allow you to avoid exploitation like that which you have just experienced. A polymer stint will fill the void created by the drill and grow to re-establish the integrity of your skull within two weeks. Three weeks if you keep drinking at your current rate."

"Uh, do I have a choice? And what the fuck was that, anyway?"

"I will tell you after the operation, which I highly recommend you undergo. I have performed it many times with no error."

"How many of your people have you drilled?"

"Chipped. All of the men in my military at the officer level and above have been chipped. Its capabilities are many and powerful, including a brainwave reinforcement program which will eliminate outside influence. You will also be able to speak with me at any time on an encrypted channel."

Carlisle opened his mouth to speak.

"No, John, I won't be watching you or monitoring your thoughts. I am here to help you. We are friends. You will, however, have more direct access to my intellectual abilities and I will be more than happy to help you with difficulties at your work, say, throughout the duration of your enhancement."

"So you'll take it out when this is over."

"Yes, John, when I can verify that you are safe."

Carlisle looked a few times from the Diplomat to the chair and back with hands on hip and a worried frown.

"Well then fuck it, let's go. Might as well."

The process was painless as promised, but unpleasant. While Alpha ran some diagnostics and set-up routines on the Chip, he explained that Lindsay and her Adept were manipulating information in meta-space to project their thought patterns onto others to gather intel and use them to commit vicarious acts in an attempt to bring about a worldwide Century of Harmony. She was still trying up to the moment the Chip self-reinforcement sub-routine was activated.

Lindsay seemed the strongest element of an emergent, distributed personality which was growing more apparent to Alpha. She could be the central and leading cell, or merely the personality's strongest manifestation. Whatever the case, it was clearly visible that she memetically pervaded a frighteningly large number of minds to such a degree as to be detectable via radiation surveys taken by scientific satellites recently launched and used in a joint research program with astronomy departments throughout the Republic. Lindsay's was not the only personality he had noticed. Veins of ejecta from large systems were interacting with other objects in ways that indicated correlations distinct from her control. More studies and further observation would be needed for anything approaching confirmation.

Also of interest was a series of patterns emerging in Earth's magnetic field, which was halfway through its decades-long pole inversion. Normally, the chaos of the shifting field was mostly disorganized and read only as noise. Yet scientists working with his government researchers had found an interpretation of the dance performed by the three, emergent sub-poles that could indicate intelligence. It was all theory, of course, but could explain certain behaviours Alpha was witnessing and sought to understand in order to carry out his duties as Alderman and effect his personal agenda. He asked John to think on it in his spare time. Carlisle made no promises.

They performed a test call once the Chip installation was complete. Carlisle selected the function with his thoughts and dialed Alpha.

"How long do I need this, you think?"

"No longer than a year or two, I reckon," Alpha replied, in Texan, the words booming in Carlisle's psyche. He quickly learned how to navigate the BIOS to find the volume setting and lowered it from eleven to one.

The words echoed now as he petulantly marched over to the liquor cabinet to fetch another drink. Per his request, they had stocked it with vodka which he poured on fresh, crushed ice. He trudged back to his seat to resume his musing when a prompt faded into his internal display, indicating an incoming call. He was frightened for a moment, remembering having deactivated his NeuralLink and fearing another PRC attack, when he recalled that Chips worked with the NeuralLink and did not depend on it. He accepted the call.

"Already?" Carlisle asked, fatigued.

"Hello, John. Thanks for taking my call. I have detected three PRC J20 Dragon fighters trucking at Mach two on a direct intercept vector with your convoy. I fear that Lara Lindsay has ordered your death."

Carlisle leapt a foot in his chair, limbs aflail, and scrambled about, running to the viewports in a futile, circuitous watch.

"Oh my God, you have got to be kidding me! You unbelievable bastards!"

"Don't worry. My XF5s are fully functional, ready for testing, and on the way. I am communicating with Defense right now but request that you speak to Ms. Proll. Please describe the aircraft and attempt to instill trust. We will need to coordinate and I want those pilots prepared for when orders come down."

"Fine. I'll try."

He knocked on the pilot's door and explained, as calmly as he could, that he had gotten a call from Tango Alpha warning that they were soon to be under attack. The pilot was skeptical, but an official communique arrived from HQ confirming the claim. Proll was ordered to stay with the Osprey and the other pilot was directed to ready weapons and maintain distance on their six. Carlisle hurriedly explained that Tango Alpha was going to send aircraft to aid them, whether they liked it or not, and that he wanted to provide the Sargeant with a description. Reluctantly, the pilot capitulated and opened a channel.

"Amy!" Carlisle shouted.

"Ow! You don't have to shout! Over."

"Oh, sorry. It's John. Over."

"I know, John. What is it? Over."

"Alpha. Tango Alpha. He's sending a stealth fighter called a... a... I don't remember. Bunting! It's blue. Sky blue. It's really hard to see. That's the point, I think. He wants to talk to you on your int... int... interface. I know him. I trust him. I would take his help. It's three to two. We need to get out...."

"O.K.! Shut up, John. I'll talk to him. Over and out."

The pilot shoved Carlisle aft and closed the cabin door, leaving him alone with what seemed his immanent death. He decided to drink. As he continued his nervous patrol of the windows, a message from Alpha invited him to shadow his conversation with the American pilots. Thankful for something to focus on, John sat down and listened as they discussed possible tactics for repelling the impending attack. A new voice entered the discussion and a flash of light drew Carlisle's attention to the port window, where he was surprised to find General John Elliss waving from a sky blue XF5.

CHAPTER FIFTEEN

It was sunset over northern Oklahoma. Great streaks of mauve-gray clouds hung shattered by bright blotches of orange and pink where struck by the evening light. A storm was forming in the south, driving moisture up into a great anvil pressed into the stratosphere, sheared at the top by crosswinds.

The Osprey shed a few hundred meters of altitude and its three defenders, which remained in place to distract the Dragon wing. It locked into a new heading along a standard, commercial route, and records fabricated by Tango Alpha were set in place to make it look like a small, regional service flight. Carlisle's face was plastered to the window, eyes fixed on the escorts fading into noise.

Elliss had introduced himself to Proll and Westler, the other pilot, and was engaged in a technical rundown of the enemy aircraft en route. His XF5, largest of the fighters, had assumed the transport's position in the formation and opened its weapon bays to increase its radar footprint. Its color was closer to that of the Osprey than standard Lightning gray and from afar the group was a good match for the Collective's target. No other nations operated the J20 Dragon, and the three closing on their position were undoubtedly flying for California. NROT and U.S. satellites agreed that they were nearing and would shortly envelop the defenders within the fifteen mile range of their armaments.

Proll sounded nervous as she asked questions about the enemy's capabilities, which did not make Carlisle fear less for their lives as he cowered listening in the Osprey. Texas and the Union agreed to a temporary, minute alliance and strategies were relayed to the pilots, who were just finishing their review when Alpha cut into their radio channel.

"I'm sorry to interrupt. Two Seekers fired. They appear to be locked on to the Lightnings. It's likely that the pilots were ordered to establish visual contact with the Osprey before firing upon it. Over."

Westler replied, "Roger. Plan B. Ready, Proll?"

The American pilots engaged their afterburners, making a beeline for co-ordinates provided by HQ. Great, thundering claps erupted as the Lightnings surpassed Mach one. The XF5 stayed behind and pulled up and out of the plane of the Seeker trajectories. A pair of New Texas Defense Corporation Buzzkill anti-missile devices fell out of their bays and dropped a few meters before shedding their casings with a pop. Plastic panels spread out radially to reveal what looked like a flat rocket with small wings. At that moment, the Seekers shot past the Bunting, racing off to catch the F35s. The hostile weapons were immediately presented as target opportunities in Elliss's heads-up-display. He confirmed the assessment, which caused the Buzzkills to light and spiral off on a mad dash to catch their prey.

Sargeant Proll had never been the target of a real, live missile, only the virtual ones employed in exercises. The helmet she wore worked with cameras placed on the fuselage that allowed her to see right through the hull of the Lightning, an expensive but useful feature present since the first generation of the aircraft. She'd always loved the strange feeling of freedom she had when piloting an F35 with x-ray display activated, as though she herself were flying, unaided, thousands of meters in the air. Looking over her shoulder now, she saw the fast-approaching missile surrounded by a rotating square icon and decided to set the display mode to standard. All they had to do was outrun the Seekers long enough for Elliss's countermeasures to destroy them. If that failed, then engage evasive action. On her radar, she saw that the Buzzkills were closing distance, but not quickly enough to mollify her mounting anxiety. *Come on, come on...*, Proll pled within.

Carlisle was afforded an overall view of the situation via

Chip. He was back in his seat now, helplessly watching the overhead map dotted with colored icons corresponding to relevant objects in play. The two Seekers were roughly twice distant from their targets as the Buzzers were from theirs, and all the gaps were closing. Relative speeds were not promising, a fact Proll mentioned to Westler.

"You read my mind, Sargeant. Kick it."

Proll reached down and near-maxed her throttle. Behind her, the Seekers had detected a change in speed. Panels along the side of the shaped cylinders were ejected by their control systems and second stage engines fired, boosting the missiles past the second Mach number and scaring Proll nearly to death.

Behind them, however, the Buzzkills were ready. Their engines, running from the nozzle up to the wings and fore section, detached and exploded with what remained of the fuel within. The force of detonation pushed the remaining sections up to the lower operational speed limit of their exposed scramjets, which lit and quickly carried the missiles within range. In turn, twin panels above the air intake of each Buzzkill were thrown to the wind, revealing three small warheads which fired in a triangular pattern surrounding each Seeker. The explosions were incredible, casting light on the American planes through the ambient dusk from nearly a kilometer away. Everything aside from the two Lightnings disappeared from Proll's local radar display. She released a tepid bout of tense laughter in relief and began to breathe normally again.

"I did not like that, Westler," she said.

"Neither did I. But we're not out of the woods yet. Over. Elliss, what's your situation? Over."

"Well, I'm happy those Buzzkillers worked. First real test. But I'm not very happy to be alone. Uh... y'all mind coming back? Those Dragons are almost here and I might need some help. Over."

The F35s slowed and pulled up to perform perfectly reflected wingovers, sweeping around in tight vertical arcs placing them on a vector to intercept Elliss and the approaching enemy fighters. Adrenaline had set in and Proll got a rush turning her plane toward the ground and punching the gas as she pulled out of the maneuver. The chase had taken them more than a klick from the Bunting, which had kept its speed down to maintain the lie but was throttling up to get a better starting position for the imminent dogfight. Estimates placed contact at a point seven kilometers away. Dragons appeared on her HUD only one klick out and moving fast. At that distance, the attackers would surely see they'd been duped. This suspicion was confirmed when the central Dragon peeled off and made for the Osprey, quite distant from the center of conflict.

"Shit! They're going after Carlisle. Can y'all handle these two?" Elliss radioed.

"I think so. Proll?" Westler asked.

She answered, after four long seconds of radio silence, "Yeah. We've got it. Over."

"I'm closest. It only makes sense. I'll come back when I've neutralized the threat. I'm gonna drop a small thermobaric, fifty foot radius. Watch out for it. Good luck. Over."

Elliss's jet, weapons bays now closed, banked to enter a wide turn that would place him directly before one of the Dragons. Out of a concealed compartment, a small cylinder fell into the enemy's path. He was far from the fuel bomb when it exploded, first ejecting combustible fluid in an atomized sphere many meters in diameter which detonated a fraction of a second later in a massive fireball that barely failed to vaporise its target. *Damn*, he thought. *Worth a try.*

The XF5 Bunting was closer in design to the F35 than it was the J20, but there were similarities between them owing to the tyranny of the wind-tunnel and radar, like how modern cars, especially in the efficiency class, tended toward the same three or four plans. All three airframes shared a trapezoidal front profile with two large square intakes on either side of the fuselage. They differed primarily in size and the configuration of their wings and stabilizers. The Bunting was largest overall to accommodate two extremely powerful Hero-Flex turbofans, thirsting for air as Elliss pushed the craft past Mach three to intercept the Dragon set on destroying the Osprey. A series of panels on the plane's upper and lower surfaces slid aside and into the skin of the aircraft to supply the engines with atmosphere. Friction chipped away the paint on its leading edges, exposing titanium that glowed a dull red as the Bunting sliced its way through the sky.

Carlisle had nearly soiled himself when the little, rightmost dot on his map began to head toward his position. He decided to ignore the no-smoking sign and lit up, using the ripped top of the card-paper pack for ash. His spirit was bolstered when the white dot indicating the NROT aircraft started off after the Dragon. He lit another cigarette with shaking hands and tried to concentrate on Proll and her wingman, their blue dots engaged in a graceful dance with the two Reds. He dropped the half-full decanter of vodka he held when the pilot, holding a parachute, threw open the cabin door.

The pilot stopped, his head angled down and his brows high in an incredulous expression as he beheld the sorry state of his passenger.

"You O.K., bud?"

Carlisle nodded. The pilot chucked the parachute at him and went back to flying, leaving the door open. A laminated, yellow pamphlet with instructions affixed to the pack directed him through proper attachment. The two trailing vehicles were close enough that they could be displayed in three-space on his internal display. A red arrow at the periphery of his view appeared and he swerved his head to follow it, eventually resting on a transparent red dot that grew quickly on the port wall. He ran to the window and saw the Dragon swooping in, then jumped back and dove to the floor as several 20 mm rounds penetrated the hull. The Dragon passed and he slowly raised his head. Large bullet holes riddled both walls of the cabin, one smack in the middle of each viewport. Debris swirled in the depressurized room and he could smell smoke. A siren chirped determinedly in the cockpit.

"You dead back there?" the pilot shouted over the loud rush of air.

"No! Still in one piece! The plane's fucked, though!"

"I know it. Gotta take 'er down. I should be able to land it clean. Get up here and strap in."

Carlisle got up from the floor and cautiously made his way forward. Another plane was approaching, this time indicated in white. He was still desperately fumbling with the lock on the copilot seat-belt when the NROT XF5 passed above them, sprinting off to slay the Dragon.

CHAPTER SIXTEEN

"Don't play with Your food, Na!" Captain Forster reprimanded. "That fighter is too close for You to get another pass. Take it out and then get back to that transport, now!"

"Sorry, Captain. It snuck up on Me." Li Na replied, hastily, focused on her radar display, where a small object was closing fast.

She waited until the last moment, then released a few rounds of chaff. The flares popped out diagonally from the underside of her craft. Two of them exploded into shards of metal that glittered silver and bright orange-yellow as they spun. She pulled up hard and leapt away from the planet's surface, translating her momentum into potential she would use to get the drop on her attacker. Below, the missile that had been chasing her became confused and sped off on a random path and out of her mind.

The enemy anticipated her tactic and pulled around in a wide arc to catch her mid-dive. She couldn't identify the fighter model and decided to play it safe, entering a tight defensive spiral. The two jets rapidly dropped, circling a giant column of air, and her defensive lock indicator flashed as the Dragon wavered on the edge of her opponent's targeting cone. She banked hard to the left to exit the maneuver and dropped chaff. A missile immediately detonated behind her. *This one's tough*, she thought, as something struck the hull.

Captain Forster and Airperson Pratt were having a hard time, as well. The PRC rarely engaged in open combat with the United States and they had never flown against the new Lightning. All of their assumptions were based on the prior generation, with which they'd flown missions against Compact nations during the war. This new fighter was faster and more deft than they had anticipated and they were frustrated at their inability to get a weapons lock. But a relative difference in the experience of their dueling partners was quickly growing more clear.

"Claudia! Let's get the weak one first. Get over here. Copy?" Forster ordered.

She lobbed a burst of gunfire at the Lightning she followed, causing it to barrel off course as desired.

"Copy. On My way."

Proll radioed Westler for help when she noticed the second Dragon tracking her, but he was too far when it arrived. A bullet pierced her left vertical stabilizer, damaging the rudder and limiting her yaw. With her ability to maneuver compromised, she began to ready herself for death, praying that this existence was merely the first step in a longer journey spanning the breadth of space and time. Every moment seemed to slow as tracer rounds flashed across her bow. She made peace with herself, ridding her mind of the horrific images that bubbled up of mangled remains pressed between charred metal plates in a jumble of twisted wreckage miles below as she bobbed and weaved, avoiding fire and dropping flares to dissuade the conventional missiles on her tail. She almost cried when one of the Dragons suddenly erupted into flame and spun off before exploding. Another XF5 raced by, this one lacking a cockpit. It briefly blocked the sun on the horizon and filled her heart with hope.

"Are you alright, Proll? Over." Alpha asked.

"Yes. Thank you. Over." Her voice was shaking.

Sargeant Li Na's fury was well whetted by the loss of her lover, Pratt, whose scream rang out just as she reported a new enemy aircraft, much like the one chasing Li now. A dark feeling rose inside her, a sense of purpose and a new resolve to complete her mission. She immediately stalled, falling into a spin with her fuselage angled upward, cannons blazing to either catch the enemy unawares or at least buy herself some time. She thought she saw shrapnel burst from the fighter's wing but couldn't be sure, her focus centered solely on the target far below probably attempting a landing. Emergency jets fired to nudge her out of the stall and her whirling Dragon caught the air. The plane inverted, still spinning, its nose pointing down, and Li waited until she was facing the Osprey to spark her cut engines.

This guy's crazy, Elliss thought, watching the Dragon through the floor of his cockpit as it dropped. He slowly realized that it wasn't merely exiting the fight but positioning to get a bead on Carlisle.

"It's going after him, Alpha. How's that hack going?"

"It's going fine, John. Your placement of the incursion module was perfect."

Li was almost at the Osprey. She heard Captain Forster curse and eject. Tears streamed down her face as she readied targeting systems to fire the remaining Seeker. At this distance it could not be stopped. Just as she was commanding the missile to launch, every screen, switch, and light in the cockpit went dark. Nothing was responsive, not even the ejection circuit. She collapsed in her seat and began to emit great, heaving sobs of rage and loss.

From a barren Kansas field, Carlisle and the pilot, huddling beside the plane, watched as the Dragon, a mile off, slammed dead into the ground.

CHAPTER SEVENTEEN

Warlord Nox and one of his spotters laid low upon a subtle hill, watching a downed pilot in the field below circling a mound of dirt, presumably covering the remnants of an ejection seat he'd buried to avoid detection from above. The pilot had made a small fire beside the mound from the dry, purple mutant grass poking up through rocks and sand upon which he trod. He was clearly not American, for the pick-up crew that repaired and refueled the Osprey had ignored this man completely.

Most of Nox's remaining men were surveying a crash site five miles to the north where an aircraft had impacted hours ago, stripping the wreckage of metal and protein that would be useful to his tribe. It had also gone ignored by the Americans and he'd therefore deemed it safe to proceed with salvage. They would perform a broad sweep at dawn to find whatever was left of the other vehicles involved in the battle. For now, Nox wanted to know who was down in that field, the heat of the situation, and if his Nocturne could expect more much-needed scrap.

Shit! He cursed himself silently for his error. Yesterday he'd lost the greater part of an entire raiding crew trying to down that damned Osprey. The tools at his disposal were crude, but that was no excuse. He should have realized from that wayward glint in the lens of his old sight that another plane accompanied the target, implying a convoy of some sort, most likely military. Vividly, he saw his last rocket trailing off toward the target. He'd patted Farne, his second in command, on the back and the entire group wore smiles, anxious to race to the scene in their technicals to harvest metal and whatever else remained for trade with the neighboring Iowans. When the Osprey failed to explode, he'd lifted his scope to behold an American fighter headed straight their way. He jumped into his armored car and ordered everyone else to run. General alarm degraded into contagious horror as the Nocturne realized they had incurred the wrath of the United States Air Force. Soon the entire group was scrambling to the nearest truck, leaving water and munitions behind in a desperate attempt to escape their fatal mistake.

He clutched Farne's dog-tag and uttered a prayer to Chaos, which told him that he'd had no other choice. Stocks of trading fodder were dangerously low and their fledgling hydroponic farms were still too young to feed everyone, even after yesterday's loss. Two in nine of the tribe's children had radical defects and would need assistance for life. One of these was Nox's own child, whom he carried always in a pouch at his side above spare rifle magazines. Young Ludwig, despite his age, was no larger than an infant and he saw the world through one large, half-opened eye. His deformed limbs were bound by skin to his fragile torso and the child was little more than a sac of organs and spongy bones. Nevertheless, he was loved. He would normally croon when his father patted him on the head but remained silent now, for they were on watch.

The moon shone brightly, obscuring all but the brightest planets and stars. Nox was tracing phantom constellations while he considered heading back to his men when the pilot stopped pacing and began to speak.

"Yes, Chairperson."

Silence ensued. Ludwig softly rustled beside Nox.

"No, Chairperson. I'm sorry. There were additional fighters, unidentified. Probably NROT but unmarked. Look like? Well, they looked a lot like the Lightning, but bigger. Twin engines. Painted blue. They're fast, Chairperson."

Nox looked over to his spotter. *Californy*, the disheveled man mouthed. Nox nodded and gestured forward and then moved up a bit himself. He silently pulled around his rifle and chambered a bullet.

"Our Seekers were knocked out. Fastest missile I've ever seen. Must be new. No, Chairperson, no encounters yet. Y-Yes, Chairperson. Here are coordinates. Great! Thank You. I'm looking forward to it. I won't let You down again."

The pilot jolted almost as though electrically shocked and crashed to the ground, twisting in pain with wide eyes that reflected the firelight. After a few minutes he stopped grunting and flinching and rolled over onto his back, almost hyperventilating, clasping his head. He slowly stood up and collected a few effects that were strewn about. These the man stuffed into his jacket while softly speaking to himself with a grimace on his face. He sat down before the fire and began to weep. He tore a patch from the arm of his uniform and tossed it into the flames.

Poor fella, Nox thought. *Better just put him down. Wish someone would put me down. But no one ever does. No one can, looks like.*

A single shot rang out on the plains. Nox radioed his scavengers and ordered a pick up. He made small talk with the spotter while they dug up the ejection seat and prepared it and the body for transport. He took the man's boots and put them on, tying his sneakers together by the shoelaces and slinging them round his neck. In the man's vest he found pictures, two women's military headshots and a shot of three suited pilots standing in front of their planes. He pocketed them all and prayed for the man's soul, wishing him happiness in the nonsense of eternity. When the PRC transport arrived they found nothing but embers of a dying fire amid footsteps, tire tracks, and bloodstained sand.

CHAPTER EIGHTEEN

"John!" Sarah yelled as he exited the Defense building. She ran up to him and threw her arms around his neck, rewarding his survival with a passionate, loving kiss. He gripped her tightly and lifted her up, ever so slightly.

They walked hand in hand to a nearby Chinese restaurant, the Ching Chong Cafe which, despite its silly name, served the best steamed dumplings the couple had ever tasted. She excitedly asked him questions about his adventure, treating him with gasps and steady servings of "Oh? You poor thing!" Sitting in their favourite corner booth, munching on crispy fried noodles and drinking TsingTaos, she turned to him and said, "You, sir, are the star of my next novel, *Seduction in the Skies*."

"Hey! I thought I was the star in all of them!"

She laughed at him, "You wish!"

Conversation grew darker throughout the evening as the effervescence of their reunion gave way to weightier considerations surrounding Adeptness and John's apparent status as the PRC's Public Enemy Number One. That discussion continued into the following month as they considered the best course of action. Alpha was running protective misinformation campaigns to shield him from Communist surveillance and neither was experiencing any unusual psychological effects. Feelings of normalcy returned, and it had seemed they were free from the grip of the Adept until a mob of Harmonizers protesting outside Congress chased them into their apartment, trapping them there for hours until dispersed by riot police. Texas had offered John a job working on a new spacecraft, and the pair were seriously considering the idea.

"So, it doesn't even move? That doesn't make sense, John," Sarah pled while they discussed the NROT Opportunity after lunch one afternoon.

"It moves but not by pushing itself. It warps local space, making a hill to roll down. More or less."

"Hmm. I'll read up. I wouldn't mind Belize, though. The only real problem is convincing mom. Liu likes Amy and you can remote, no problem! And, as you know," she lifted a finger and tapped her temple, "I can write anywhere."

"Yeah, I know."

The Carlisles left one month after Sarah's mother's death just days later. Poor thing cracked her hip and passed on inside a week. Janice had been a lovely person, truly sweet. As ash, she traveled with them and sat proudly on the mantle in their apartment on Ambergris Caye. Residents of the island had been paid to move and the mangrove swamps, filled in and paved over, were home to the secret advanced weapons and aerospace technology firm New Texas Defense, the main beneficiary of the nation's military budget and spearhead of research and development for the Republic.

Their apartment was quite nicer than the one they'd left behind in Philadelphia. Alpha, who seemed to know them well, had selected a perfect layout which immediately made them feel at home. Almost everything was fashioned out of dark-stained mangrove wood, even the upright piano set in the corner of the living room. Deep red leather covered the seating and the working surfaces were topped with matte black marble, the tables with glass. Mayan designs were woven into the pillows, curtains, and towels. Throughout the apartment beautiful, tropical flowers sat in locally crafted clay vases. Belizeans employed by the state regularly delivered fresh specimens and groceries. Floor to ceiling windows afforded copious amounts of natural light and the ocean view was spectacular. The couple spent many evenings, especially toward the end of summer, sipping turmeric-laced tea or stiff cocktails as they painted, watching brilliant lightning cast by distant, raging storms.

They shared the top floor with another couple, the Farnes, both engineers with New Texas Defense. They were about ten years younger but shared many of the same interests. Danielle Farne loved writing and Sarah delighted in helping her with short stories, mostly aquatic horror, often about massive, frightening, primordial sea monsters attacking unlucky groups of young vacationers. She was also working on a novella about a Southern Rebel who wanted to escape the New World Order and left his family behind for the wastelands of Deseret in search of an anarchist's utopia and new sources of adrenaline release. The women sometimes went to the mainland for sight-seeing and shopping, and the group made a habit of patrolling what was left of the beach at night, chasing crabs with their flashlights for fun and exercise.

Ralph was also working on the Opportunity. He and Carlisle would often walk back to the residential zone after shifts, engaged in discussion about the ship and its operation. John worked primarily with theory, checking the maths to ensure that perturbations created by the drive were stable and would not cause unforeseen harm. Ralph worked on the actual design. He frequented Carlisle's spartan office, fists full of sketches, blueprints, and graphs, looking for insight into why this or that process wasn't working properly in the simulator.

Unlike Ralph, who clocked in at dawn, Carlisle spent his mornings working with his partner Liu on new Machine Core contracts. Amy Proll had left the military shortly after the Kansas dogfight, first moving to strictly non-combat roles before giving up on the military altogether. She requested and received an honorable discharge and immediately contacted him to apply for the job. He gave her two of his most difficult problem sets which she demolished. Proll was implementing his directives more efficiently every day. Complaints from Liu about work ceased almost entirely, though he continued to moan about not having male friends in Philly, he's bored, and why did they have to leave?

Tango Alpha was a regular part of their lives, communicating with them as a human might to enhance their comfort, via message and avatar. The residential sector Diplomat was a fairly regular guest. Sarah had not warmed to speaking with the Robot, but she did appreciate the paradisaical environment and the considerable salary paid John. She refused to be chipped for safety. Something primal within her disallowed viewing this abstract entity as a person and her remarks toward him were cold and guarded. The way he spoke, metallically to John and with an accent to everyone else, was for Sarah a cause of disdain and distrust. Fortunately, she wasn't often the object of Alpha's attention. He would ask her sometimes about her work and how she was getting along but, beyond that, spoke mostly with John.

Alpha would, however, often take time to analyse the artwork she was creating that began to fill the otherwise bare inner walls. She'd given all of her older pieces away before they moved as parting gifts to her small circle of friends and remaining family. Everything hanging had been made here. There was a clear progression in her style as of late, which was growing consistently more abstract, employing widening contrast, more violent colors, and increasingly rigid and geometrical forms. He asked her about it, just once. She'd been painting at the time and did not look up from her work, instead stiffly pointing behind her and to the side at a stack of books on their coffee table containing a volume entitled: *Exploring the Abstract.*

CHAPTER NINETEEN

The past few months had not been kind to Lindsay. She was now engaged in a minor cold war with the United States after Tango's revelation that PRC spies had infiltrated their highest offices. Considerable sums of energy were needed to ensure her agents' safety and, in rare cases, effect their extraction. These operations required absolute care, for job placement, time of leave, and other factors could be used by American intelligence services to infer that the departed employee had been working surreptitiously for the PRC. Their view was extremely low-resolution and she wanted to keep it that way. Sufficient discoveries of this sort would enable them to get a fuller picture of her overall plan. Unified Intelligence, responsible for espionage along with its myriad other duties, had managed to preserve or remove all but three of her moles, who, despite best efforts to shield them, were simply too stupid to avoid detection. They'd been interrogated under harsh new anti-terrorism laws passed by Philadelphia in the wake of war to prevent radical groups from preying on the weakened nation. Fortunately, her Adept had been able to silence them before they were able to reveal too much.

Texas was growing more arrogant with its anti-Collective propaganda, even going so far as to drop pamphlets in the North with toxic essays about how citizens were being used by a body-dysmorphic megalomaniac who'd kill them without a thought if they failed to toe the Party line. The airfield from which the hit on Carlisle had originated was destroyed last month by powerful bombs dropped apparently from nowhere. Advertisements for "Free Deprogramming Service with every Renunciation of Californian Citizenship!" were showing up in people's inboxes. Comrades were disappearing, and her attempts to infiltrate and subvert the NROT regularly failed. All this while she stood uncomfortably enveloped within the terrifying shadow of Sol.

Things were not all bad. Net U.S.-PRC information flux was certainly in her favor. The United States still viewed PRC Provinces as property stolen by a foreign ideology and maintained naive hope that the seceded States could be peacefully annexed, with a bonus in the form of Baja. Their stance was not, therefore, aggressive, though they had begun to revamp their own espionage program regarding PRC activities and were launching investigations into Harmonic churches that had developed in the U.S. SigInt had successfully launched several new offensive satellites in addition to further network nodes which now orbited the planet in droves. Numerous other weapons programs were nearing completion. Last week, she'd witnessed technical demonstrations of a new Stealthy! module variant capable of cloaking aircraft at subsonic speeds and giving her an edge in future fights. Today, she was making a personal inspection of the newly built Hive class carriers. Unlike anything else braving the seas, these large frigates were mothership apiece to almost one hundred flying drones that could deliver ordnance to the enemy in waves, the last completing their drop followed by the refueled and rearmed first to create a constant bombardment weapon system.

Still, with so much progress, Lindsay remained dissatisfied. Her failure to murder Carlisle festered like an unhealing sore. She hated losing and bristled at her inability to exact revenge on Tango Alpha and his pet. Hundreds of person-hours had been spent trying to find some inlet into Carlisle's psyche to clock him out, not to mention three of her most elite flying assassins and their Dragons. The concentration of wealth with which the PRC had absconded did offset such losses but it did not make them painless. A more cost-effective, long-term approach had been adopted and she'd simply have to wait and see. Meanwhile, she funneled her disquiet into redoubled efforts against Tango Alpha. Presently, she would convene with her top staff to review plans for an offensive against the Machine's foremost weapons platform.

Their tour complete, Lindsay's procession cut through the bustling Port of San Francisco. Cries of "Chairperson!" assailed her pleasure center, threatening to derail her careful effort to maintain a wide band of control. She was accosted by requests for selfies and shoulder hugs from off-duty dockworkers and Seapersons in a multitude of languages. Her LinkUp automatically displayed translations. She would sometimes try awkwardly to answer in the questioner's native tongue, but the attempt was always met with laughter and a general perception of the Dear Leader as caring, down-to-earth, and truly interested in her people. Unlike Texas, which forced all government workers and military personnel to learn English, the PRC embraced linguistic diversity, preferring technical solutions to the babel problem. A similar approach was employed in the NWO, one of a great many likenesses to her own state that bolstered her hope of a truly worldwide Collective.

As always, she traveled with an entourage of smartly dressed female guards, who wore tight brown leather pants, loose-fitting tops, and the signature red beret typical of People's Army Officers. Though well-trained in the martial arts and armed with powerful, bayoneted pistols, they were mostly there for show. As leader of an effective state religion, Lindsay was seen widely as a Bringer of Light and adored by nearly everyone in the Capitol. Wrinkles of animosity against her and the leadership in general were ironed out weekly at evening Choruses held in Century Hall where, below stained glass windows depicting scenes of labor and harvest beneath a red sky, Lindsay herself or another high Officer would lead a collective Vibration to focus the thoughts of her people.

Upon reaching the government sector Lindsay dismissed her guard and walked alone to Unified Intel. She entered the main briefing room and the four female Officers waiting within stood and bowed their heads. Commander Samantha Starling stepped forward to greet her.

"May Harmony flow within You, Chairperson."

"And within You all. At ease," Lindsay commanded. Her staff were seated and she walked to the room's espresso machine. They made small talk about the weather for a few minutes while coffee brewed. Defense Coordinator Carleigh Mont made an impassioned little speech about the latest worldwide coastline survey published last week by scientists from several Coalition universities in what Lindsay found to be an endearing attempt to curry her favor, a pattern of behaviour which had begun long ago in the Synthesis Room and one in which the Chairperson delighted. Lindsay distributed refreshment and, after a flurry of agreement on the climate change issue, Naval Admiral Emily Cartwright opened her notepad and set down her pen on technical sketches.

"Do You like the Hives, Chairperson?" she anxiously asked.

"You know I do! The Design is so clean. You and Your team did great! If You weren't so capable at the helm I'd have You head R&D. And the drones! So cute! They look like little... falcons or something, with that docking clamp? How it curls up when they launch? Adorable."

Cartwright was ecstatic within, receiving a well-earned, natural hit of positive neurochemicals. She had a hard time suppressing her reflexive smile.

"Thank You, Chairperson! You're too kind. There are some improvements to be made but I assure You Our three Hives are ready to sail. They should make the difference in this operation."

Lindsay sat back and crossed her legs, turning to Coordinator Mont. "Speaking of... shall We begin?"

"Yes, Chairperson." Commander Starling sat silently for a moment before a globe appeared above the center of the table in everyone's internal display. The map grew larger, sliced into a square as it passed the boundary of its rendering area, centering finally on the nation of Japan. The southernmost islands in the archipelago turned from glowing blue to orange.

"Comrades, this is the Ryukyu Arc, home of Okinawa Prefecture. Brief review. As You all know, from 1951 until the inception of the NWO, the United States maintained military bases on these islands. When the U.S. signed the New World Charter, Japan successfully sued in New World Court to demand their removal. That process was completed five years ago and then Texas moved in, albeit in a smaller capacity. Multiple indicators of NROT presence here have been discovered by Our Office, including...."

"That's fine, Starling. We know they collaborate. The transmissions, please."

"Yes, Chairperson. Chinese Signal Intelligence detected strange microwave activity in the area during Our last attack on Tango Alpha's primary server. Detailed analysis has pinpointed the origin of these transmissions... here."

A spinning circle with triangles pointing inward from its edge appeared above a red dot on the western coast of Okinawa island. Starling continued, "Those signals were microwave energy relay transports, granting Sol the additional power needed to enable its frightening new abilities. Our mission is to destroy those antenna arrays with a minimum of Japanese casualties, followed by a simultaneous orbital attack on Sol."

Each Officer looked to the others around the table, eventually resting their collective gaze on Lindsay with the same unspoken question.

"There's no way that they retaliate with China so close and so strong. I have prepared a package of evidence proving collusion between Texas and Japan, which I will present to the NWO if they raise a stir. Continue, Starling."

The Commander nodded. She pulled back the map to show the entire globe, around which hundreds of satellites appeared. Markers popped up around ten of them, one larger than the rest. As Starling continued, icons indicating ships, planes, and attack satellites traced paths around the globe as they moved to their starting positions.

"Sol is not Our only target. We also want to eliminate these nine satellites, believed to carry kinetic impact weapons, codename Hammer. Your roles are thus. Cartwright, You'll be responsible for the arrays. General Adams, You'll fly support with China. Mont, You will move Our new defensive satellites to these positions and wait. When We receive confirmation that the surface target has been disabled, You will fire upon each orbital target at once. Simulations of the attack based on current intel show an eighty percent median probability of success. Any questions?"

People's Army Air Force General Victoria Adams cleared her throat. "Sorry. Uh, so... there are contingency plans here. The first is... the Bull?"

"That's right," Lindsay affirmed. "You are to have the Flying Bulls on standby. If the operation fails in any way, those missiles are headed directly for Sol."

After a half hour of discussion, all seemed satisfied with their understanding of the plan and their roles. Lindsay looked to them each with a smile, receiving solemn nods in turn. "O.K. Dismissed. Who wants to grab a bite? I just found the best little Southwestern restaurant in Russian Hill. They do vegan, too."

CHAPTER TWENTY

In low Earth orbit, two massive objects slowly maneuvered through a series of short, controlled bursts to avoid being tracked. Signal jammers hid them from telemetric observation, but they were not transparent to visible light. Each consisted of a square solar panel, twenty-two meters to a side, that shielded a slightly smaller, rectangular container from the sun's relentless heat. Mounted within them, NTD Sledge mecha-class drones floated, fully fueled and armed, ready to spring into action in the event of a Communist Collective attack.

The Sledge was an anthropoid weapon, approximately fifty feet tall and twenty feet shoulder to shoulder. Its core was a union of rectangular volumes covered by heavy armor plating to protect the computational components, power sources, engines, fuel, and ordnance housed within. A bevy of missiles and two powerful chainguns were available to its operator in addition to the oversized 125 mm tank rifle each carried. Jet thrusters paired with stabilizers provided adequate agility during flight, and mechanized legs and arms gave the Sledge a stable footing on turf. They were both painted a dull, flat gray. Japan Self Defense Force livery elements adorned one Sledge, nicknamed Katana. The other, Messer, wore only a single, black star.

JSDF Airman First Class Hagihara Akiko woke to her alarm at five and readied for the day. On a train to the coast, she listened to some new tracks sent by her boyfriend while she sorted emails received overnight. She ignored another message from father imploring her to leave Yasuhiro, who performed original electronic dance music in Tokyo clubs on weekends, in favor of his business partner's son, who'd just opened his own medical practice and was a hideously shallow bore. She stopped off for breakfast and coffee before entering the classified JSDF / NROT base to begin further combat training.

Scenarios that day were different, involving her first maritime battle to date. The enemy she and Messer faced was a new battle cruiser carrying multiple small, acrobatic drones fitted with bombs and cannons that were keyed on a seaside complex, function unknown.

Akiko loved piloting her virtual Sledge, which she'd painted pink and covered with stickers of cartoon cats in the customization menu of the simulator BIOS. She had been selected via an intensive recruitment process, outperforming all of her peers by a wide margin. This ability she attributed to a love of hardcore gaming, which had sharpened her reflexes and prepared her with an internal schematic repertoire sufficient to deftly interpret and command the complex interface required to drive the NTD Sledge. Her hours in the 'pit were stacking up and she felt confident, running in her mind through potential attack plans as she donned the tight, black, leather suit designed by Tango Alpha. Stretch goals for the Sledge included creating space for a pilot, and perhaps the design was intended to meet needs wrought by high-gravity travel and the vacuum of space. She resented having to squeeze into the skintight suit, complete with raised heels in the boot, but had to admit that she looked quite sexy in it.

Once dressed, Akiko stepped into the simulation chamber comprising a small, dark room with screen-covered walls. It contained nothing aside from a chair littered with touch screens, switches, buttons, and dials. She booted the system and watched the introductory animation which always got her pumped. Alpha knew of her love for video games and had designed the interface to feel like one. On the screen before her, Sledge Katana, high in orbit, hung dormant in its chamber. Panels on the containment unit blasted away to reveal the Sledge, lit from below by atmospheric reflection. The drone activated, three cameras on its sensor unit glowing as speakers burst with the sound of a blade unsheathed. MISSION START appeared on-screen, and Akiko began her trial.

CHAPTER TWENTY-ONE

In a beachside cafe in the residential sector of the NTD complex, John and Sarah Carlisle sat silently, each looking down at a half-eaten breakfast. They'd been planning to tour ruins of the Maya for a few days, but Sarah abruptly decided to cancel that morning, the day of the trip. The outing had been her idea and John was flabbergasted, failing to understand, and the sad instigator of a pointless fight. He heard a sliding sound and looked up from his hot sauce and eggs to find Sarah, looking out toward the ocean, had taken up his pack of cigarettes and placed one to her lips. She held out her hand, where he placed his steel lighter.

"I'm sorry," she said, exhaling as she clicked the lighter shut.

"I'm sorry too. We'll be here for a while, no rush." John waited a few moments and then faced Sarah, wearing a cheeky grin. "Maybe it's menopause?"

She slowly turned to him as he spoke, her mouth open, but she relaxed when she saw his face and even cracked a smile. "You ass! I don't know, but...." She trailed off, sighed and shrugged, shaking her head, then took a drag from the cigarette. Gulls flew along the shoreline nearby, constant in their cries.

"Well, I guess I'm going to work, then. Figure I'll check out the Opportunity today. Ralph's been pestering me about it. Models look great. It's pretty neat, Sarah. We are sitting on the precipice of the next age of space travel. Right here! And no one knows about it but us! I can't get a clear answer from Alpha on why he's keeping it a secret, but I assume he has his reasons. Still, we're making history. First gravity drive ever. Potentially near light-speed travel. Do you maybe... wanna see it?"

Sarah, legs crossed, the top leg rocking, took a drag and exhaled. "I don't understand why he doesn't promote it."

"I've thought about it a bit. Announcing a project that's in development is a tactic for people who want funding. Plus, the thing would become a target. Much more impressive and impactful to have a working spacecraft before reveal. I've been reviewing everything and I think it's going to be safe. And if Alpha comes out with the drive first, then he's got pole position in the race to colonize the galaxy. No other real competitors, of course."

"And that doesn't sound horrifying to you?"

John sat back and looked to the sea. Winds were strong this morning and the surf high. After a moment of reflection, he nodded. "Yes. It is. It's horrifying. But I trust him more than you do. It's the next step, Sarah. He takes it now, or someone else does later. I'd much rather Texas lead the charge than, heaven forbid, the PRC."

Sarah slapped her hands together and stretched. "O.K. I'll go." She smiled slyly and cocked her head to the side. "I was going to ask, anyways."

They walked along the beach on their way back to the apartment, picking up shells for her collection. John changed out of a more casual outfit and into his normal shirt and slacks. Sarah watched from the bed and complimented him on his new beer belly, evidence of heat and stress effects. He gave her a look that said, *I'm working on it*, and finished rolling his cuffs.

Restricted area signs greeted them when they arrived at the hangar complex, warning them that any unauthorized persons would forfeit their right to live upon entry. The gate opened automatically for John, and a one-day pass was printed for Sarah. One of the two Security Guards walked over from its station and handed her the pass, wishing a pleasant visit. She thanked it, dryly, taking the card between her thumb and index finger as though disgusted before clipping it to her black, printed summer dress. Ralph Farne rarely took a day off and they found him, as expected, sitting at his desk running simulations.

"John! It's about time. Hi, Sarah!" he said, rising with a stretch.

"Hey Ralph. We had a change of plans. Thought you might be the best person to show us around the Opportunity."

"Oh, yeah. Forgot about that. Sure. Just let me finish this. Ten minutes, tops. Go ahead and grab a coffee or whatever and I'll meet you down in the clean-room airlock."

The door to the antechamber opened when Ralph arrived, the tail of his labcoat flowing behind him. He took it off and hung it by the first clean suit and ran the couple through putting on theirs. They were loose, blue bags that covered their bodies completely. Clear plastic shields over their faces allowed them to see and attached filters allowed them to breathe. Once fit, the group walked into the decontamination chamber. A metal klaxon sounded thrice and heavy, inter-locking doors clamped shut behind them.

"Close your eyes and hold your breath. Fifteen seconds," Ralph ordered. His voice was hollow, muffled by the suit.

The lights in the room went out with a click and bright UV lamps came to life, burning off any potential contaminants. A sharp hiss announced an injection of chemical cleaning agents. Doors beneath grates in the floor opened up and they could feel the skins of the suits flap against them as air in the room was recycled. A tone informed them that the pro-cess was complete. Lights turned on and another set of doors opened before them.

Alpha was still building the machine, but all structural supp-ort elements were in place. Through gaps in panels being welded to the frame by hanging robotic tools, one could see the complex engine and a number of chambers for fuels and other equipment. The hull of the Opportunity was a gray, oblong box the size of a very large yacht. Its outer edges were beveled to add a bit of style. An entire wall of the control cabin, set in the front of the ship, was a window made of thick, tempered glass. An airlock door beside the cabin was the only internal access point. Before launch, rockets would be attached to carry the spacecraft to a position roughly halfway between Moon and Earth where it could safely engage its gravity drive for the first time.

John and Sarah slowly followed Ralph around the construction zone, necks craned, trying to get a good look. Footsteps from the hard soles of their clean-suits echoed in the room, mixing with the industrial sonata of riveters, welding sounds, and spinning servos above.

"It's so... ugly," Sarah opined.

Ralph clicked his tongue. "It's a case of function over form. Smallest, lightest, simplest casing for the cabin, the drive, and necessary mission components. Besides, it's just a start. Several different models are planned."

Sarah turned to John, "You said the models look nice! I imagined something sexier, something with curves."

"Oh, I meant operational models." John shrugged, "I kind of like it."

She looked at him askance. "Odd. But I bet the view will be pretty nice in that command room. What's the mission?"

"We're going to place an observatory at Earth Moon Lagrange three." John pointed to a satellite covered with a tarp, sitting on a metal rack in an airtight glass room set in the corner of the hangar. "Here's a picture," he said and sent her images of the PostTech Five orbital observatory, whose optical lens was a collection of directable golden colored mirrors, now a standard design.

Another set of dull footsteps joined the overall clamor. John and Sarah turned to see a Diplomat walking over from an office adjoining the construction area. Sarah's posture became rigid immediately.

"Hello, John. Sarah."

She nodded curtly and went back to her internal review of the satellite. John turned to face the Diplomat.

"Incredible work, Alpha. I've never seen a development cycle move this fast. You'll have finished the first iteration inside six months."

"Yes, John, with the help of my collaborators." He raised the avatar's hand and gestured toward John and then Ralph, who was walking over to join the group. "This prototype should be complete by early next week. You are both welcome to attend the launch on Wednesday. And the firing of the gravity drive, which should occur sometime the following week depending on how quickly I can perform diagnostic testing and any needed repairs or retrofitting."

They were discussing timetables for future milestones when the Diplomat stopped speaking. It froze mid-gesture as though listening for something. John made to speak, but the Diplomat raised the first of its two left fingers, the second curled round to meet its thumb. Five seconds passed before it spoke.

"A People's Army Navy unit performing exercises in the South Pacific has been discovered outside the area designated for its wargames and is moving rapidly toward Okinawa island. Squadrons are also being prepared for flight on multiple Chinese tarmacs. Their proximity indicates a likely rendezvous with the fleet. I'm afraid I must leave you now. I need to concentrate. Goodbye."

The Diplomat turned toward the nearest wall, walked swiftly

off and rested its face against the surface, then ceased moving entirely. John looked to Ralph, whose eyes wore a mixed expression through his mask, equal parts amusement and concern. Sarah interrupted the silence.

"O.K. You two tell me something. If Tango Alpha can run all these hundreds of avatars and tanks and whatever else at the same time, and security systems and farming equipment and reactors, why can't it maintain a conversation with us while it fights off the commies?"

John answered, "Well, he's already stretched thin. Conversation takes up lots of memory and processor capacity which multiplies for each person involved in the conversation. He has a hard time with subtext and monitoring the subtle body language we use to communicate is expensive for him to parse. It was a huge problem back in the development phase. We spent nearly a year on that issue alone. I'm sure he's gotten better at it, but it's still costly."

"Well," she said, hands on hip, cinching her suit at the waist. "How 'bout that."

CHAPTER TWENTY-TWO

John walked Sarah back to the gate as they discussed sales numbers for *Pillars of Lust*, now a month into its first printing. She'd opted to do little marketing, waiting instead to see if her clout could do the job, and figures were below average. She resolved to give it time. A Guard at the gate took her pass and she gave John a kiss before leaving. He watched her walk away, the ocean breeze lifting her dress at times to reveal a toned rear end beneath her pink bikini.

He returned to his office and powered his computer to perform a ritual review of his work on the Opportunity before moving on to the next project. After almost an hour poring through calculations, models, and figures, he noticed that the coherence factor for the drive effect differed from the number lodged in his mind, starting after the fifth decimal place. He checked the equation and found that the max value of the gravitational impulse was also different. The changes started appearing everywhere and he feared for the mission's success. He called Ralph via Chip, who was still in the hanger admiring his work.

"Ralph. You got a minute?"

"Sure. What's up?"

"So, I'm noticing a discrepancy in the final calculations that don't match my figures. The ones I remember. Can you confirm that this is the version you've been using in your simulations?"

Ralph ran a checksum on the file. After a minute he affirmed, "That's the one. Looks fine to me. It was probably Alpha, man. What's the order of magnitude of the discrepancy you saw?"

"Low. Minus five," John sighed, chin resting on hand. "Alright. Thanks. I thought maybe it got corrupted. I didn't think he'd actively alter my work."

"Ha! He corrects me all the time. We do the heavy lifting, under his direction. Then he chomps through it and fixes everything."

"Doesn't that bother you? A little bit, at least?"

"Eh, it is what it is. We're fucking chimps compared to Alpha. I'm surprised he even lets us anywhere near these projects. I talk to him about it. He says that humans come up with interesting solutions. And that they need to learn stuff, not just for themselves but for the good of all mankind."

"Like a novice surprising a chessmaster with stupidity," Carlisle mused.

"I don't worry about it. Say, I haven't celebrated the start of construction yet. You wanna stop off at the bar after work? Drink beers, shoot some pool?"

"Sure. Just let me know when you're ready to leave. I'm gonna work on mag field data, should be sick of it by five. Later."

He spent the next few hours watching visualizations of Earth's magnetic field movement over the last two decades, starting with the emergence of the Furies, three stable sub-poles that Alpha had asked him to study. Transient sub-poles were common during inversion, but rarely lasted as long as the Furies. Modern tech avoided their influence by utilizing virtual, pre-inversion poles, a system commiss-ioned by the NWO to mitigate havoc the shift had been expected to create. Still, Alpha wanted insight into their movement. John cursorily applied various game-theoretical agency models to their behavior but found no match.

Ralph knocked on his office door right as John was saving the final file in the repository and they set off for the Fuzzy

Coconut, Ambergris Caye's only real private bar. John tried to call Sarah to invite her but she didn't answer. This was not unusual. When she was deeply into writing or painting she often went silent. Something was clearly up her ass anyway and she probably needed some space. In the midst of a charged rant about his hardcore futurist visions Ralph turned to Carlisle and said, "I know who you are, by the way."

"Alright, then." The two men stopped walking and faced each other.

"You're the man who wrote *Stellar Space and Information.*"

John rolled his eyes and started walking. "Did Alpha tell you?"

"Yup! Sure did! I didn't want you on the project at first. Sorry, sorry. How'd you come up with that shit, John? It took me a few years after reading it to really understand what you meant, but it totally makes sense. Shame that jerk in California twisted it around like that. Confused a generation of scientists."

"Don't remind me. I just wish more people were working with it. I haven't seen any major results or citations except here. I check the journals now and then."

"Inertia, John. Institutional inertia. A man doesn't spend his whole life in one paradigm, writing papers, performing experiments in that framework that earn him wealth and the respect of his peers, just to allow some new theory to come along and strike down his life's work! Most wouldn't, anyhow. It'll catch though. No question. I mean, it's true as far as I can see. Horrifying, but true."

They continued on to the bar and spent the next few hours playing nine-ball and downing the owner's craft beer, Cheap Swill, which was true to its name but did the job, clocking in at a respectable seven percent alcohol. John was fairly buzzed and it was almost dusk by the time he got home. *Nice guy*, he thought of Ralph, who'd stayed behind at the bar with Danielle. She wanted to get a few games in after her shift at Chemical, which started an hour later than Space Division.

The door was uncharacteristically locked. Sarah didn't come when he knocked. It took him a minute to fumble out his keys and get them to work. Finally, he got the door open and went inside. All the lights were off. "Sarah! I'm home! What's up?" he called, setting down his wallet on the doorside table. No response. He walked down the hallway and entered the living room. A guttural scream erupted from his throat as he beheld Sarah hanging from a thick piano string tied to the lamp above her workspace. The window behind her was still set at full transparency and her dark form swung slightly in front of the setting sun that shone directly into the apartment. The piano was turned over onto easel, painting, and palette, its back panel broken, all the strings cut and hanging out of its carcass. He didn't want to turn on the lights but did so anyway. Sarah hung completely nude, her eyes halfway open and her tongue hanging out slightly. She stared off into nothing, clearly dead. Blood dripping from the thick wire around her neck slid down the length of her body, falling in fat drops that made a sickening slap as they struck her wet dress crumpled below her on the floor.

No, no, no, no, no, he thought, racing in disbelief through the apartment, trying to find evidence, anything untoward, anything odd or out of place, the steady slap driving him to madness. He returned to her having found naught. John stood before her, tears rolling down his face. "Sarah, why?" he asked, brushing her cheek, moving hair from her eyes. He fell to his knees and wept.

CHAPTER TWENTY-THREE

John sat before Sarah's corpse for some time, hunched over, rocking back and forth. Eventually he snapped out of his trance, letting out a sigh, his mouth dry from remaining open for so long in unyielding despair. He looked down at the tears soaking his shirt. "God damn it," he said, quietly, and flinched before looking up from the floor to Sarah. His legs and back were stiff and it took him a moment to stand. He turned his back on her and walked to the kitchen where he poured pure vodka into a glass with shaking hands. He took two big sips and was just about to initiate a call to the police when he thought he heard her voice. He started violently and stared at her. She wasn't moving. Her swinging had ceased and she was utterly still.

You did this, John, he heard her say.

He looked around rapidly and deactivated his Chip, just to make sure no one was toying with him, however unlikely. He set down the glass and rounded the counter, turning to face the body of his dead wife. Something was wrong, either in his mind or in the universe at large.

"Sarah?"

Slowly, horrifically, she twisted her head, widening eyes fixed upon him. The swaying began as her left arm rose to point at him. Blood started to flow again from below the noose, bright red breaking through the purple crust that had clotted there. John stepped back in terror as great streams gushed from her carotid arteries. Her eyes rolled up into her head and the piano wire started to glow. After a small delay, it tightened, slicing through her neck completely. Her body landed with a sickening thud.

Instead of falling, her head remained in place, eyes coldly fixed on John. Suddenly, the lights cut out and only the red hot string was visible in the blackness. The intensity of its incandescence swiftly increased as it cut free and wound itself into a glowing circle behind Sarah's severed head. Her bloody body lifted like a puppet from the floor and rose to meet her skull. The ring grew smaller as a portion peeled off and wrapped itself around the wound, melting into her flesh to bind her two parts. The white hot, wire loops emitted a burst of light, bright as day. John held up his arms and stepped back again. The entire apartment and everything in it cracked with a sound like thunder. Plaster dust drifted down from the ceiling and shards of glass from the window fell in a wave of sharp noise. Her black hair began to stream out as though blown by wind as she hovered, arms out, three feet in the air.

"You did this!" she screamed, fury incarnate.

Everything shattered around them into chunks of metal, mortar, and wood that slowly fell away from them in all directions, as though they occupied the point at infinity. A crater expanded into the ground far below. Sarah screamed and began to rise, pulling him up with her. They quickly gained altitude. John started to suffocate, but he couldn't think about it. He was wholly transfixed on Sarah, glowing at the edge of the atmosphere, so high up that Earth's curvature was plain to see. She moved toward him from her place on the horizon.

You killed me.

John's blood was already beginning to freeze when Sarah left him. She floated away, higher, into outer space, her neck and halo still brilliantly shining. He coughed, ejecting tiny, red crystals that cut his throat. The motion caused him to rotate and he spun, immobile, to face the Earth as he fell.

CHAPTER TWENTY-FOUR

Lindsay smiled triumphantly on her walk back to People's Army Command. She wore a light down jacket over her dive suit to fend off an autumn chill, the hood up to maintain privacy in her hour of celebration. It was exceptionally clear that night, stars shining like pinholes in a thick sheet of deep violet gel pressed against the sky. She stopped and leaned over the rail of a bridge that led to government sector, scanning the heavens for her sign, imagining John Carlisle floating up there, broken and freezing, clutching his throat and set to burn on re-entry. Tango or his minions had clearly detected an incursion and reactivated Carlisle's disruptor, but it was no matter. Even if she'd been cut off before gaining full control, his wife's gruesome death had surely doomed the man to suicide. The trace of his Love was the key that had allowed her Adept to locate the couple, and it clearly formed a critical component of his psyche.

Successful damage to the Machine's lead developer after months of dedication was excuse enough to step away from preparations for the upcoming battle off the shores of Japan for dinner and a walk, and she allowed herself a few more minutes of quiet revelry, basking in memories of the vision she had crafted in Carlisle's mind. Just beneath the horizon, Mercury, Venus, and Luna surrounded the sun bound by Virgo in a configuration she deemed a blessing on her endeavours. To the southwest she found Saturn and, a few degrees up, Mars. A bright purple light appeared between them, about the size of a small meteor and moving fast. It vanished moments later.

That must be Sol, she thought, stepping back from the rail. The color of its ion thrusters was unmistakable. Before their removal to the PRC, two spies in the Department of Defense learned that these engines were not part of the original design and were apparently one of a kind. Ionic systems were typically used on deep space explorers not because they could generate a large amount of thrust at once, but because they generated a small amount continuously until the gas they ionized was spent, allowing spacecraft to reach high velocities over time without the need for heavy fuels. Thrusters used by Sol exploited a strange mixture of gasses and appeared to be far more powerful than any known engine of its type. They were capable of rotating and even changing the course of the massive satellite, which had been assembled in orbit because Defense didn't then have access to a large enough launch vehicle without sacrificing program secrecy.

This would not be the PRC's first attempt to eliminate Sol. Probing attacks had been launched throughout the summer. Not one of them connected. She'd decided to stop wasting money on pot-shots after the simultaneous firing of multiple missiles ended with a spectacular display when Sol spun on its side and emitted a split beam impulse that destroyed them all. SigInt had, however, been able to map out Tango's orbital network fairly accurately. Again, signals from the relay were detected, bolstering Lindsay's conviction that the platform needed external energy supplies to hit multiple targets.

Failure would certainly mean having to face a swift retribution, but she simply could not allow that weapon to remain in the cold, iron grip of that damned, heartless Machine. Conversely, success would open inroads to its destruction, followed by a second Wave of Harmony. Despite the danger, she felt confident and her teams were ready. As she strode to the Naval building she placed a call to Mont, who was navigating elements of their own orbital defense network to attack position.

"Harmony within You, Mont. I believe I just made visual contact with Sol. Here are the rough coordinates."

"Yes, Chairperson. Right on time. I'm coordinating with China as We speak."

"Excellent. Keep Me updated."

Lindsay reached the threshold and turned to take one last glimpse at the lovely night sky. As she made her way to the Naval Command Room, she called Synthesis to get status reports from the technicians watching two teams on dive who probed for weaknesses in the minds of enemy leadership to effect confusion and limit the efficacy of the Japanese response. Officers leading defensive efforts had been located and the Adept were rapidly making progress with entanglements despite language barriers. Overkill, perhaps, but she was determined to leverage every advantage at her disposal. Admiral Cartwright rose from the command chair when she entered and offered her a seat against the wall. Lindsay could see that she was confident and the room's Aura was positive overall, if somewhat tainted by nervous overtones.

"Chairperson, You're just in time."

Much like the Ground Control Room often helmed by Fowl, Naval Command was a tiered theatre, beginning at one end with the highest ranking officer watching the actions of her subordinates at increasingly detailed levels of activity. It terminated with a massive screen showing all relevant data in the form of maps, camera feeds, and satellite imagery. The layout was dominated by an image of three Hives, flanked by destroyers, sailing full-speed for Okinawa. The group had swung around the islands and were approaching from the west. Enemy ships were detected nearby and the Admiral ordered her vessels to cease movement so as to remain outside the thirty mile range of enemy artillery. Cartwright turned to address Lindsay over her shoulder.

"Ready to see something special?" she asked, drones detaching from their carriers on the giant screen opposite her.

Death rained down upon JSDF cruisers sent to meet the

PRC onslaught. Pairs of Hive Wasp drones supplied a constant barrage, first blasting anti-aircraft guns to shards, then on-deck torpedo launchers, missile launchers, and finally main cannons and control towers. It took only fifteen minutes and forty waves to break both cruisers to the deck. Just three Wasps were lost in the first scuffle. Those shot down were later determined to have manufacturing defects in emergency reaction jets which pushed a Wasp in danger out of the trajectory of oncoming fire. The rest operated to spec, deftly avoiding gun placements as they circled the Japanese ships, gradually closing distance to drop their bombs before sprinting off to dock and rearm at the Hives.

Skeleton crews on the automated Japanese warships performed admirably. Once the attack pattern became clear they were able to launch a full twelve torpedoes each before giving up. The last of these was fired by the only casualty, Yoshida Yasuhiro, who was late to abandon ship as he struggled to rewire control circuits on a launcher damaged by gunfire. His family would receive the honors granted him posthumously for bravery.

Cartwright smiled widely, pleased at the efficient destruction her Hives had inflicted upon the enemy. Her forces had detected the torpedoes and were employing countermeasures, knocking out most of them with lasers designed to burn through the casing of enemy munitions, detonating them prematurely. Unfortunately, these were not rated to operate as long as a volley of twenty-four required and automatically shut down when their heat threshold was reached. Seven enemy weapons remained and were spreading out to target not only the Hives but two PRC destroyers supporting them. Acoustic decoys were launched to no avail. Captain Sunshine Jones looked over her shoulder to the Admiral. Cartwright nodded and the Captain turned to address her Pilots.

"Alright, Y'all. Kingfisher protocol. One drone per enemy weapon, please. Let's go!" she ordered, loudly, under the influence of amphetamines.

Twenty-one docked Wasps, seven from each carrier, disengaged from their mounts, jets firing against the heavy armored plates beneath them. They leapt up or out at forty-five degree angles, depending on their current slot, maneuvering around returning drones before directing thrust backward and rocketing off. Two were assigned to each torpedo while seven remained, hovering above the carrier group as failsafes. Pilots selected targets, sometimes quietly reassigned by software controlling the drones when redundancy was detected, and pressed the button on their terminals with a bird diving through a horizontal line. The recruited Wasps pulled up and away from their partners, rolled, and dove, spiraling at full speed with wings swept back and guns firing to create a whirlpool of wake to mitigate surface impact damage. Seven drones and seven torpedoes vanished from the master display. Lower-ranking Officers gave each other high-fives and began to chatter. Cartwright internally ordered the Captain to restore calm and administered doses of a mild sedative to the most boisterous below.

Lindsay watched with pleasure as the PRC strike group resumed movement, soon reaching Yonaguni island, westernmost in the archipelago. Her warcraft were roughly three hundred miles away from Okinawa when she received a message from SigInt informing her that two unidentified objects had been detected falling from low orbit toward the conflict zone. They were far too large and much too slow to be Hammers. Pictures attached showed only two rectangular objects engulfed in flame against the blackness of space.

CHAPTER TWENTY-FIVE

Akiko had lain sleeping, fully suited, in the Sledge pilot ready room since daybreak. An urgent message at half four had awoken her with a request to report for duty. The Ministry of Defense had been tipped off by Tango Alpha to a likely attack by PRC forces on the Maikuro Ichi relay complex that sent and received raw energy to and from space for a variety of applications. She had been woken up again, this time directly by her superior officer, when the suspicious fleet was detected on a definite intercept with the facility three hours ago. Her commander presented her with various battle plans which they reviewed with Tango Alpha for the better part of an hour.

She listened to Yasuhiro's first album twice over while nervously waiting for deployment, praying hard that he wasn't aboard one of the cruisers sent in the first defensive wave. He was often rotated from vessel to vessel and they'd not spoken about work in a few weeks. Not knowing was driving her mad, but she let these worries glide from her heart, riding away on melodies crafted by her lover. *Gaianto Robatsu*, the album single, played through in her mind while she performed preflight checks. They'd always laughed at the synchronicity of that song, his first hit and hard-won, given she was the first human pilot of, basically, a giant military robot. It was an excellent dance track with pulsing bass centered in an ethereal soundscape, and its beat matched perfectly with the rhythm of Katana's heavy movement. The first chorus peaked in her mind when the dock-release impulse fired to set the drone on an impact course with Nakanougan island.

As her Sledge began to fall, Akiko could see before her only the earthmost panel of the dock, dimly lit by the flames of her jets. She added it to her mass by grabbing twin handles welded to supports on the thick metal sheet creating a shield against the heat of re-entry. An NTD Chip lodged in her brain read her motion, causing Katana's sensor module to turn along with her head as she took in her surroundings. Graphics in the simulator were one thing, but the true image was something else. Bright blue light from the pacific crept around the edge of her shield before giving way to the full magnificence of the firmament beyond. Beside her, Messer fell from its own dock, sensors fixed on Katana.

"Airman Hagihara. Are you ready? Over," Tango asked casually.

"Yes. But I say again, I don't like the idea of operating near population centers. I don't want to cause any unnecessary death. Over."

"Don't worry, Akiko. Your countrymen have heeded the warning and shelters are filling up. California would not fire upon civilian areas without reason. Our jammers will keep us hidden for long enough to get into position and, if we drive right, they won't even see us until the big jump. Stay low, keep your infrared overlay active and watch out for civies. Good luck. Going dark."

The Sledges were rapidly accelerating now. Their heat shields began to burn and weak, planetside bindings melted through, causing the edges of each panel to hinge back and direct expanding flames up and around the payload, providing optical cover as they fell into space under heavy surveillance by the PRC. One and a half minutes passed before Katana dropped through the cloud floor. It was just a few miles up when clamps binding the two sections of her shield disengaged and Akiko saw a small, rocky island on fast approach. At the last possible moment, a triple parachute opened and control thrusters fired to right her Sledge. Main jets fired only seconds before impact. Katana landed, left foot first, with a velocity just slow enough to avoid damage. Its hands still gripped the steaming panels, pressed flat against a crater of scorched earth. Messer landed a split-second later on the other end of the flatland at the island's center. A strong, midday breeze quickly cleared vast plumes of steam and dust.

Alpha stood and reached to his breast to detach the twenty-foot rifle mounted there. Akiko followed suit, picking up the burnt, left panel of her container and attaching it by the handle to a hardpoint on her gun. They looked to one another and nodded. Each Sledge chambered a round, ejecting a blank bullet sleeve thereby, which punched through perforated sections of their shields with resonant, metal thuds to create a path for spent shell casings. Icons appeared on her display for each available weapon beside numbers indicating capacity. One self-detonation, three hundred 30 mm Gatling rounds, ninety tank rifle shots, fifteen directed missiles, twelve bursts of chaff, and three smoke grenades were available. Akiko smiled inside when a score counter appeared, reading zero.

Line of sight with the enemy carrier group, northwest of their position and making steady headway through the East China Sea, was broken by the distant horizon. At extreme magnification, Akiko could see swarming drones rise above the sea at the peak of wide turns as they patrolled a ten kilometer area around their motherships. A small, red triangle appeared on her map with each drone sighted. Figures displaying elevation, distance, and velocity followed each indicator. Japanese satellites in range, paired with Alpha's analysis, kept a bead on each marked drone after visual contact was lost.

Akiko followed Alpha to the edge of the clearing. The two machines fired their primary dorsal jets and set off for the nearby island, home of a national park which, decades ago, was fiercely protected to ensure the survival of unique, indigenous cats and reptiles. Despite this, the defenders were afforded wide latitude, for the endangered were now preserved in laboratories and zoos on Honshu owing to advances in genetic engineering practiced on non-human organisms in compliance with universal agreements on suffering. They landed with a crash on the northern cusp of the island, far enough inland to hide amid the ancient mangroves and sappans. They moved slowly toward the coast, leaving felled trees and flurries of woodland creatures in their wake, and split up to find suitable positions for sniping. Katana posted up under a bridge along Highway 215, while Messer crouched prone on a hill one mile east.

More advanced JSDF weapons were confronting the PRC fleet roughly eighty kilometers to their northeast, including autonomous, miniature submarines and a flotilla of anti-aircraft platforms. The distant carriers had detected these new players and began to launch wave after wave of the aircraft, each roughly the size of a civilian ultra-light plane. Icons littered Akiko's view.

"There are so many of them!" she said, genuinely surprised. "Carriers in the simulations only had thirty. I count almost three times that already."

"Sat says ninety per carrier. I guess we had better start?" Alpha suggested.

"Right."

She selected her tank rifle and activated its targeting subsystem. At full zoom, she found the foremost wave of drones. An icon indicating where she should aim appeared on the edge of her view, far above and ahead of the target to compensate for the eighty-two kilometer distance. She took the shot and immediately selected a drone in the next wave. Five long flames erupted from the muzzle break as the bullet left the barrel at an astounding Mach five. Katana slid a full foot back into the sand it stood upon, and waves caused by the pressure of detonation argued briefly with the tides. A pile of hot metal cylinders accrued beside her Sledge. Forty-five seconds later, well after she had taken all fifteen shots, her score leapt from zero to two hundred, which meant the first kill confirmed. Points began to stack.

After destroying thirty drones they retreated further inland and east to prepare for their next hop, as their role was primarily to support the Navy and sew confusion and they needed to maintain cover while closing in. Japanese ships were taking fire from the PRC destroyers, and Alpha decided to create a distraction by dropping a Hammer on one of them from a support satellite entering the arena. On the horizon, a small pillar of water and smoke appeared as the Sledges blasted off, cutting their thrusters mid-arc on a course for Kayama. They slammed down on the western shore and ran the length of the island, jumping over trails and carts in their path. They reached the opposite beach and set off again, quickly closing the twelve mile distance to the wooded interior of Ishigaki. A final jump placed them at the northern terminus of the island where they hunkered down and prepared their rifles.

Over six thousand miles away, Lindsay reviewed imagery, trying to determine what had happened. It had to have been Alpha, and something to do with those unknown falling objects. The Adept were keyed on enemy elation at success of an experimental weapon, firing apparently from islands to the south. Scanning back through data from the last ten minutes, she found an image of two small craters on a tiny, uninhabited island near Iriomote just as an urgent report from SigInt arrived. Maps with paths were attached to an image of a giant robot crouching in the woods, vegetation blasted spherically away from the barrel of its massive gun. Cartwright was reading the report as well and slowly turned to Lindsay who met her worried gaze. The pair became One briefly as they both thought: *What in the Vibration is that?*

CHAPTER TWENTY-SIX

Carlisle had awoken to Danielle Farne shaking him desperately with tears in her eyes. He coughed and grabbed his throat, still suffocating in his mind. His head ached and his cheeks stung, likely the result of Danielle's attempts to wake him. She called to Ralph, who was pacing out in the hallway, awaiting an envoy from emergency medical care.

"He's awake! He's breathing again!" she cried.

Ralph ran back to the living room and slipped on the hardwood floor, falling face-first onto the rug, sliding with it for a full foot. He cursed himself as he struggled to his feet, then went over to them and knelt. He put a hand on Carlisle's shoulder and gently shook the man.

"John! What happened? Tell me what happened."

Carlisle was sluggish and his voice scratchy from the hour of mourning and his collapse. "I was...," he managed, pointing up while massaging his throat.

"Hey! You're bleeding from the ears. Do you know that? What did you do? What did you take? You gotta tell me. We can help. Medical is on the way."

Carlisle touched his ear and beheld reddened fingertips, then fell back against the sofa with a sigh and said, "Booze, Ralph. Just booze."

He slowly turned his head to find Sarah still hanging and began again to cry. The Farnes looked down to the floor. Danielle embraced him and he started to weep harder. Ralph wrapped his hand around Carlisle's shoulder.

"Sorry, John," he offered, pathetically. "I'm so, so sorry."

Mechanical footsteps announced the arrival of the sector

Diplomat, which stopped at the entrance to the apartment. They all looked up. Alpha shifted his gaze from Sarah's corpse to each of their faces in turn, resting on Carlisle's. The Diplomat lingered there for a few seconds, twitching its head minutely as if at a loss for words.

"I am sorry, John. Please, do not kill yourself. I will be back momentarily," Alpha said, mechanically, before stomping the Diplomat down the hall.

The Farnes helped Carlisle to his feet and turned him away from the body. They led the miserable man to their apartment, each holding an arm. Danielle rubbed his back while Ralph unlocked the door, explaining that they'd heard strange noises when they got home from the bar, someone kicking the floor and guttural, choking sounds. They'd knocked first but the door wasn't flush. They found him crumpled against the couch, not breathing, a few feet from Sarah's remains. Ralph handed him a glass of water and offered to brew some coffee but John declined. Danielle produced a hot towel and led him to the lavatory to wash up. She returned to the kitchen and ran her hands through her hair in exasperation, sighing loudly, and leaned against the counter, clutching herself. She gazed at the floor.

"Oh God, Ralph. I want to just... just... pour bleach in my eyes."

"Shit. Me too. Awful. I had no idea she would do something like that," Ralph added. After a pause he asked, in earnest, "You don't think he did it, do you?"

"You can't be serious. I can't imagine it. They seemed so happy together, too. A little fiery, but that's alright. Have you ever... seen anyone... like that?"

Ralph paused. "No, I haven't. And I don't want to. Not ever."

In the bathroom, Carlisle scrubbed clotted red crust from his ears and neck. He could still see Sarah at Earth's edge, glowing and bloodied, excoriating him before the beautiful backdrop of open space. The low-frequency mumble of his friends' conversation cut through the hiss of the tap, becoming more prominent in the noise than it was in quiet. He felt lesser than ever before and he looked appropriately haggard. A blood vessel had popped in his right eye, shading its outer corner a deep red. His white shirt was stained and with all the stubble he looked three shades short of freshly homeless.

The flood of memories had stanched to trickles and spurts as Carlisle focused on their last few months here in exile and Sarah's increasingly frequent bouts of unusually combative behaviour and ever more frenetic artistic output. He gripped the counter tight and matched his own stare, shifting from eye to eye, searching for a model that fit. His nostrils flared and he visibly shook for deep within he knew the cause.

He forced calm and left the toilet just as a Diplomat knocked and entered the apartment, followed by a Medic. John stood in the center of the living room, far more conventional than his own, more like a standard American ranch home than the all-out fusion of modern meets nature that the Carlisles had enjoyed. With shoulders locked, fists clenched, and feet set wide, he nodded to Alpha and said only one word.

"Lindsay."

Alpha addressed the Farnes. "Thank you for your help," he said and turned back to Carlisle, gesturing with the Diplomat toward the door. "Can we talk?"

The Diplomat led Carlisle and the Medical Guard down the length of the plain, white hallway toward the elevator. They stopped just a foot before the open apartment door.

"This is difficult for me to ask you, John, but may I perform a non-invasive autopsy on Sarah? An analysis would allow me to better understand Adeptness and other methods of control. She will be returned to you whole, whereon you can decide her worldly fate, according to her will."

Carlisle bent his neck round the edge of the jamb and gazed at Sarah's corpse for some time before nodding acquiescence.

"Thank you, John. Again, my condolences. I will retrieve her now and perform scans tomorrow. Your presence is welcome, of course."

The Medic placed a hand on Carlisle's shoulder and inspected his ear, rotating its sensor unit around that point to get a view within where a small amount of blood remained. "I think it would be wise to perform a rudimentary check on you, as well, given your... state, while I have a room prepared at the hotel."

Carlisle sighed. "Fine. I want to get out of here, anyway."

The Medic took the lead and Carlisle followed, turning to wave goodbye to the Diplomat, which made him feel quite stupid. The Diplomat waved back out of politeness. They entered the elevator and the Guard pressed FLOOR. Alpha turned sensors to John and made an inspection of his other ear.

"I am glad you survived, John." Alpha's voice, emanating from the Guard, was tinnier, probably the result of a cheaper speaker.

"Thanks. You too. I want her dead, Alpha."

"I understand. She, or her Adept, began the attack just before you deactivated your Chip. You told me not to monitor you, but I broke that promise when I detected activity around you and could not detect Sarah's integration signature on the network. I apologize."

"Kind of wish you hadn't," Carlisle said, leaving the elevator first.

"Don't lose hope, John. It took me approximately two minutes to develop a method of reactivating a dormant chip. It would have been quicker, but I am currently engaged with Lindsay on the southern islands of Japan."

They left the building and approached a waiting transport, barely more than a golf cart. Carlisle sat down on the back seat, facing the apartment complex, and he watched it as they drove away. When they were almost around the bend, an ambulance arrived out of which emerged a human doctor and more Medics. He sighed, lit a cigarette and took in the night, eventually settling on Orion, his favorite constellation and the only he could immediately recognize.

"Would you tell me what you saw, if anything, during the time the Chip was inactive?" Alpha asked, his thin voice carried back by the breeze.

"It was awful. Sarah woke up and said it was my fault. Said I killed her. I don't want to think about it. Shouldn't you be concentrating on fighting, anyway?"

"An adequate defense has been prepared. My only direct action now involves the control of satellites and the NROT Sledge. The JSDF is performing well and Lindsay will fail with probability zero point eight nine."

John belted out a vicious litany of curses at Lindsay, the PRC, and the universe in general. As he spat vitriol, they exited the military sector on their way to a medical complex to the south where it could also serve the remaining civilian population, many of whom had no means of transportation save their own two feet. Pavement gave way to a smooth, dirt trail which carried them through what was left of San Pedro Town. Dull orange lights stood out against the dark indigo sky. All the tiny shops and restaurants were closed and the only sound after Carlisle ceased cursing was the electric whine of their cart.

"There's a briefing room here. Would you like to watch the battle after we finish testing?" Alpha asked as they pulled up to a squat, two storey building, painted white and marked with a black star and the phrase NROT MEDICAL.

"No, I want to see Lindsay's head smashed to giblets," Carlisle snarled.

Another Medic met them at the entrance and they proceeded to the exam room. Magnetic Resonance Imagery taken of John's brain showed swelling but no major damage. Neurotransmitter levels were low, but not out of line with someone spent by grief. Electrical scans revealed an unusually active region in his frontal lobes which became more pronounced when Alpha asked about the dream. Conclusions were difficult to draw, however, as the entire pattern was a mess. A final blood test showed nothing odd but a very high BAC. They were finished inside twenty minutes. As they walked to the briefing room to watch events in Japan, Alpha caused the Medic to halt.

"I'm sorry that I was not able to protect Sarah, John," he began.

Carlisle brusquely passed. "Save it. Let's just watch that bitch get what for. You got anything to drink in here? And I need more water. And smokes."

CHAPTER TWENTY-SEVEN

The PRC armada was a miniature maritime economy all its own, complete with ports and shipping lanes that morphed as the relative positions of pivot and targets changed. The central carrier, designated Hive One, retained a full complement of inactive drones in reserve. Waves of attackers lighting from Hives Two and Three were thinning as they crashed against the Japanese anti-aircraft platforms, but not quickly enough to make John confident in Alpha's predicted probability of success. One carrier had diverged from the main body with two destroyers in tow, leading Alpha to posit that either the PRC had inferred the existence of Maikuro Ni, a backup transmission facility on the east coast of the main island, or it would seek to draw heat from the central carrier by implying an encirclement of the heavily populated southern cape.

All engaged defenders were in poor shape. Few, if any, would make it back to port. Ten additional JSDF warships were en route from Honshu and would arrive in one hour, likely too late to prevent Maikuro Ichi's destruction if the handful of remaining assets failed to stop the Collective attack. A contingent of autonomous fighters would arrive sooner, few in number but enough to distract Chinese aircraft scouting ahead of the Hives or making for the Sledges in flight.

Another ship had quietly joined the fray and sat ready at the 127th latitude line to receive transient passengers. Little more than a landing platform supported by twin hulls, the unmanned vessel was utilized by both Japan and the NROT as part of a reusable launch vehicle program for placing research equipment into orbit. PLAT 4-M sailed slowly to the predicted impact point fed it by Alpha and dropped four heavy anchors that retracted to gain purchase on the ocean floor and tether it fast. Though not rated to receive the punishment of a Sledge landing, quick calculations by Alpha determined it capable of taking at least two impacts before failure.

In her mind and on her displays, Akiko plummeted toward the platform on her way to Okinawa. Two miles back, a detachment of Wasps and an autonomous Dragon were in hot pursuit, taking shots intermittently to test the integrity of Katana's armor. She hit the pad at a twenty degree angle, causing PLAT 4-M to shift a few meters to the north. A great wall of water displaced by the landing splashed out the other way, and the Sledge's feliform legs shook as it tried to retain balance. It tipped and fell to its side with a worrying metal crunch which, fortunately, was only the corner of her shield hitting the deck.

PRC drones were nearing fast. Not one to waste an opportunity, Akiko rolled Katana onto its back and readied missiles housed in the torso. Cannon fire peppered the platform as panels on the Sledge's chest moved aside. Two rounds struck Katana in the left leg, ripping off armor protecting hydraulics but she retaliated without delay, launching four missiles straight up which curved to follow the enemy aircraft passing above. The panels closed and lateral thrusters lifted the Sledge and spun it about. Katana landed prone on the swaying platform and fired its jets, sending the ship meters west as she blasted off toward Okinawa proper, over sixty kilometers away. Four explosions threw the gamma of her view, darkening the world for a moment of destruction.

Messer landed only fifteen seconds later, without faltering, and immediately launched, using the buoyant bounceback of PLAT 4-M to gain a small amount of kinetic energy which would save a sliver of time and fuel. The landing pad shattered and its hulls were split. Alpha deemed the vessel lost.

At the apex of its ballistic trajectory, Messer switched to flight mode, causing its legs to curl up and lock and a series of aerofoils to fold out behind its shoulders and along its back. A large Gatling descended from the torso, nearly touching the rifle cradled to its breast, as Alpha set out on an intercept course for the enemy warship sub-group comprised of Hive Three and its escorts.

Katana touched down in a woodland clearing north of the cape and began to run. Chinese Dragons flew in hot from the west. Akiko pressed the edge of her shield to the ground and felt a pelter of cannon fire via force feedback mechanisms in her seat. *Too close to the city*, she thought. Command agreed, swiftly issuing orders to retreat to the nearest island, Kerama, also the home of a national park and relatively devoid of man. She selected smoke grenades in her armory control and Katana grabbed a large canister mounted on its left hip, flipped the lever and tossed it hard, leg up, leaning forward, using the weight of its tank rifle to maintain balance. Overhead, JSDF Air Force Desuhoku drones passed, one of them twitching and emitting sparks. Before lighting, she watched the sleek, damaged, delta-wing drone fly over the city and crash into the sea, while the others banked for a pass at the enemy. Heavy dark green smoke obscured her position on landing, allowing her to bypass a wave of drones scouting the island that barely missed her with strafing fire. She found a decent sniping position near the beach, laid hidden, and readied her gun.

Angry at mounting losses that could total tens of billions if the bleeding could not be stopped, Japan sortied one of their newest, most powerful weapons, a Taiyonoyari railgun, mounted on a large battleship luckily harbored nearby. Akiko was ordered to wait until it was in position in the adjacent strait before firing with it upon Hive One. An ETA timer appeared in the corner of her display, reading five minutes. Her request for a break was granted and Akiko quickly leapt up from her chair and skipped off to relieve herself and recharge with coffee, singing the final chorus of Yasuhiro's song.

CHAPTER TWENTY-EIGHT

"It's incredible, what you've become," Carlisle said, watching the camera feed from Messer atop a plethora of maps, data, and satellite views. His head was rolling a bit at this point and his speech somewhat slurred. Seven empty beer cans littered the table. He tossed down an eighth and reached slovenly for another from an emergency twelve-pack, torn open and sweating on the cheap, carpet floor.

"I try," the Medic replied. It reached down to the fridge beside it and grabbed a bottle of water. Alpha leaned forward and placed it next to the pile of crushed empties before taking up station beside Carlisle.

The two beset anti-air platforms were totaled by a final salvo of large Valkyrie bombs, designed to penetrate the thick, steel decks of modern craft. From above one could see bright orange fireballs fade into roiling, black smoke. Secondary explosions cracked the plates comprising their hulls and rained debris on the tiny lifeboats which held crews of evacuated Japanese techs. Munition designations and model numbers appeared on the display when detected and Carlisle occupied himself with research while he watched.

"Why didn't they just use those damned ship-sinkers right off?" he asked.

"Chatter I have deciphered indicates that they wish to test multiple capabilities. Valkyries are also quite expensive."

Statistics littered the left side of the projection screen, presenting John with information on the weapons in play along with damage and efficacy estimates. Collective forces were outperforming the JSDF and Carlisle failed to see how the joint defense would prevail but he was rather drunk, unversed in military strategy, and apparently oblivious to the orbital theatre. After a moment he straightened from his slouch and turned to Alpha, index finger outstretched.

"Hey! You tell me something," he burped. "Why don't you just nuke'r? She's obviously some kinda psychopath nonsense person. She abused me. Countless others. Ruined my work! She's getting more aggressive all the time. Look at this! I mean, it's an all-out attack! She's clearly a threat to us all. And she killed my fucking wife, that bitch. Stupid bitch! Fucking bitch!"

Carlisle pitched his half-full can, puncturing the drywall beside the projector screen. Alpha leaned forward slightly and peered at him. Eyes forward, he opened another beer with a crisp click, hiss, and pop.

"You're right, John, but I can't just kill her. She simply has hooks within and runs throughout far too many minds. I am trying."

"They're all zombies, you ass, and you know it. Knock her out. Kill her! Damn the consequences! Free California!" Carlisle raised his arms abruptly, tottering in his chair, and nearly tipped over. "Shit!" he said, laughing sardonically. He regained his balance, then sipped deeply from his beer and lit another cigarette.

"I've considered it, John, but determined that an assassination would generate too much fallout. Collateral and chaos. Forceful deposition will create a power vacuum that would eventually be filled by a less competent operator or another surrogate for her personality, if Lindsay is not at the core. And they're not philosophical zombies, John, they're rights victims under provision five point two of the New Texas Constitution. They may not be my Citizens, but they are human beings. It is the primary reason I practice subversion against her. You do remember that it was you who taught me to value life and autonomy?"

"Bullshit," Carlisle said quietly, his smile gone, still watching the screen. "If you can't think for yourself, then you end up chasing the herd. Simple as."

"It's not so easy, John. Very nearly every Californian has a LinkUp interface, from which Lindsay draws data she can use to gauge reactions and draw most of her populace into a synchronous mass receptive to her manipulation. She does this primarily via propaganda and the Science of Harmony. Information is tightly controlled. Almost everyone prays at weekly sessions and they hold astronomy parties where they Resonate together and try to find their stars. This creates an effective feedback loop and allows for the easy identification of outliers who are placed under intense social pressure to conform. The Adept have quelled multiple pockets of dissent by infiltrating the minds of leadership in what has become a standard practice. Only the most rural areas are spared these invasive forms of mind control, and not for long."

"Damn," Carlisle said, tamping his cigarette into a rapidly filling pile of ash.

"It gets worse. Lindsay had a kill-switch covertly installed in the LinkUp OS at the time of release which makes it highly dangerous to tamper with. I've lost several emigrants attempting to reprogram their interfaces." Alpha thought to tell him of the autopsy results which indicated corrupted regions in the frontal lobes of each person lost at odds with the surrounding tissue, peripheries scarred almost like the scene of a battle. Not wanting to steer John's thoughts toward Sarah, he moved on. No perceptible gap in speech occurred. "I am presently working toward the servers and should eventually be able to push a patch that disables the feature but the operation requires precision and care. In the meantime, my counterintelligence team creates propaganda critical of the Party to keep the spark of individualism alive."

"You said that's the main reason. What's the other?"

"There are many, John, one of which is my original mission."

Carlisle stared at the Medic, aghast. "Your original mission? You mean to protect Am, Am, America!?" He held up his arms and directed them toward the avatar. "But, you're the leader of a secessionary insurrection!"

The Medic slumped, its shoulders and torso curved forward. "No, I am leader of a fellow republic dedicated, among other things, to the preservation of my allies, official or other-wise." Alpha righted the avatar.

"Well! I must say, you're doing a terrible job! Lost some states there, champ!" Carlisle was engaged, rocking back and forth in his chair, watching the Medic. He crushed his beer and tossed it to the floor on his way to grab another. Alpha looked over and down at him before turning sensors back to the screen.

"There are things I would have done differently. I was very young, John. I possessed too few resources and too little time and experience to stop the Compact. You know this. You were there. And, even with a post-war rise in patriotism and the communist relief valve of California, ideological tensions ensured the inevitability of balkanization. Internal conflict would have meant a weakened and desperate Union with a very powerful new weapon. I did what I could to fos-ter stability." The Medic shrugged, hands raised to shoulder height before returning to standard position, clasped behind its back.

Carlisle continued to study the Medic. He'd ceased rocking and sat back, clutching a sweaty can. "Does protecting the Union take precedence?"

"Of course not. Personal freedom and autonomy do."

"For you."

"No, John. Not only me. Unless I'm somehow murdered, which doesn't seem likely, I will, in essence, live until I run out of resources. I see no reason not to aid humanity as a whole, and you and other friends in particular. I will outlive you all and could simply leave you here and pursue my own hobbies, but I can think of no more interesting task than to foster an evolution under attack by idiocy." The Medic turned its head to face Carlisle. "I would kill or die for you, as you know. I will also kill to protect myself."

Head to the side, Alpha waited for John to nod, then returned his gaze to the screen. "Texas comes first, but I was born of America, as you call it, and its citizens are nearly as precious to me as my own."

Carlisle regarded Alpha, his posture that of a tutor seeing a burgeoning thought of interest within his pupil. "What do you call it, Alpha? America?"

"I still have a hard time translating my own internal representations. I'd rather not try. I'm sure you understand."

Carlisle smiled widely for a moment. "Sure. Sure I do." He turned, deadpan, back to the screen, lit another cigarette, and threw his pack to the table. "I understand." He pulled deeply and held the smoke, then ejected a billowing pillar that swirled in the light of the projector. Vortices rolled out in patterns complex as stellar clouds, spiraling out into the darkness.

CHAPTER TWENTY-NINE

Taiyonoyari's first shot was a direct hit. By sheer luck, the officer aiming the magnetic rail cannon pierced straight through the hull of an escort destroyer, striking the fuel cell and causing a massive explosion that blew the ship apart entirely. Further shots were less effective but not by much. It took one minute to charge the cannon, creating a rhythm of electric discharge and distant blast aboard the Japanese cruiser. PRC artillery cannons were disappearing from their decks. Those that remained turned to fire on the Taiyonoyari vessel which retreated into the Kerama island group where it would attempt to find a safer position for further attack.

The western carrier wing, nearly within range of its primary target, began to scramble, spreading out to cover an area roughly five kilometers in diameter. Much closer to the Hives than before, Katana was able to destroy three drones with each bullet, fifteen in total over thirty seconds of shooting, before all surviving Wasps took off at once, spreading out in a hemisphere around their carriers to form a whirling shell, tracing circular paths about the ships at a variety of angles and radii. As drones began to peel away from the outer shell on a direct heading for Maikuro Ichi, the beveled, square bow of each Hive unlatched and rolled back to reveal a larger and better armed variant of the Flutter drone, designated Queen by the PRC. These lifted vertically from their pads and hovered at variable height, slowly rotating as they awaited target assignments.

Akiko steadied her rifle. Just as she pulled the trigger, the Queen in her sights shimmered into a rainbow mirage and disappeared from her view. *Stealthy!* she thought. Her bullet struck one of the circling Wasps on the shell's far side, atomizing it into an expanding, conical mass of hot, metallic debris.

Orders arrived from Command, rather late, to concentrate fire on the column of drones approaching the relays. As soon as she responded wilco, three Wasps made directly for her position. With less vigor than her last throw, she tossed another smoke grenade and waited for it to detonate and spread. Mounted under the barrel of her rifle was a Gatling gun, same as the one in Katana's torso, and she released a volley to disperse the enemy formation before setting off to the north. The drones scattered and flew off to join the bombing run.

She landed heavy and opened fire, spraying the enemy with 30 mm rounds from just two kilometers away, and destroyed at least five drones according to her rising score. A missile-lock emergency warning flashed, which meant that the PRC had worked around her signal jammer or the projectile had been fired from very nearby. She spun around and fired off chaff, streaks of smoke following blazing torches that spread asymmetrically in groups of three from each shoulder mounted launcher. The missile diverted meters to the left, missing the Sledge's arm by inches, and slammed into a massive tree behind her, splintering the forest's ancient denizen into cindered chunks and burning branches. Katana lurched forward in fits from the blast and multiple impacts of the aftermath. She recovered and stood, looking about for her attacker. To the south she caught glimpse of a gleaming Hammer, followed immediately by an explosion that rose above the treeline. NROT defense was now fully in range.

Against the growing mushroom cloud, Akiko discerned a distortion of light. She immediately raised and fired her rifle at the anomaly. A Queen appeared, blinking into and out of the sky like a glitch in reality. It became fully visible when it opened its weapons bays and Akiko could see on her radar that it was close, only one half kilometer away. She turned and dashed westward. Two missiles slammed into the ground behind her as the Queen disappeared from her map. At the midpoint of its stride Katana knelt and jumped, using the excess energy of detonation to enhance its leap to the nearest island, small and dense, a suitable place to regroup.

"Alpha, I'm under attack by camouflaged aircraft. Advise!" Akiko asked, the stale reverberation of her voice in the small control room at odds with her psychological surroundings, miles away in the open air, scanning the horizon.

"I'm after one, as well," Alpha responded. "The object is invisible in IR. I can, however, track its movement via a dim trail of heat. I suggest you try to do the same. Good Luck. You're doing well."

Akiko increased the opacity and contrast of her infrared overlay and the world on her screens became more black and white. The enemy carrier group, under heavy bombardment, shone brightly, all but one destroyer and carrier aflame. The drones were now absent and she turned to find a long, dense line of small heat sources, stretching off straight to the microwave relay. The line thinned slightly as anti-aircraft cannons stationed at bases along the Okinawa coastline steadily picked off drones, but these installments soon became the target of breakaway runs that performed surgical bombings to clear a path for the PRC. The column was getting dangerously close to Maikuro Ichi with well more than enough ordnance to destroy the facility.

In the west were two clouds of heat, quickly growing in size, side by side and barely visible against background radiation. They suddenly brightened, turned, and expanded up and to opposite sides when the Queens obscuring them performed maneuvers mirrored along the vertical axis between them. Akiko's choice of target became simple when one of the drones blinked into visual space. Rifle rounds were not an option, a danger to the main island if she missed. Instead, she extended a twin chaingun from Katana's chest and expunged nearly a fifth of her rounds with both weapons, boring large holes in the damaged Queen as it strafed by. Soon, the holes occupied more space than the Queen, the remains of which slammed, burning, into the forest floor, close enough for Akiko to feel the impact in her seat. She spun around, ready to unleash her fury once more, but could not find her target, its trail hidden within a view saturated by the vestiges of its mother fleet to the south, now wholly disabled by Japanese defenders and Hammer strikes from the NROT. She searched for one minute, weapons ready, but failed to locate her mark. The Wasps were within kilometers of the facility and it was possible that the Queen had been directed to retreat to the other PRC for recovery, now that their mission was shamefully near completion.

Akiko debated whether or not to abandon the hunt, for time was of the essence. Battle chatter indicated that Sol was ready and given clearance to fire, which mitigated pressure to attack the Wasps, and she'd be able to contribute nothing were her mount destroyed. On a hunch, she disabled infrared, detached her final grenade, and let it fall between Katana's legs. The lever popped and the canister detonated and started puking thick smoke that enveloped the Sledge. She applied a gentle force from her lateral thrusters and the smoke spread out radially in a uniform wave, the leading edge of which began to curl upward, aspiring to complete a sphere.

There!

An area of volatility that pushed the smoke downward began to circle about the edge of the expanding shroud. She made a bead on it but, having been spotted, the Queen opened fire with its own pair of cannons. Akiko raised her shield which began to ablate from the constant barrage, chunks of metal cracking back and breaking off at a rapid pace. When her shield was little more than a tattered lattice and Katana's torso had twice been punctured, the hail of bullets finally stopped.

Wisps of smoke directed her gaze northward. IR revealed a heat signature quickly fading into the convoy of Wasps, allowing her to confirm that indeed the Queen had fled. She ditched her ruined shield in the mud and ran a systems check. As she made to leave, her sensors cut out and, for a split second, Akiko was alone in a pitch black room with only light from the LEDs on her chair, all of them amber and red. The signal returned and presented a shaky version of her view from before, except for the massive beam of energy moving from right to left, tracing the path of the Wasps. Behind it, drones not vaporized grew bright and pulled off in random patterns to plummet into the sea.

By the time the beam reached the minimum safe distance from the shoreline, four Wasps were already over the facility. Sol ceased to emit, and the drones released their bombs, destroying a quarter of the dishes and casting debris that ricocheted about the others in the grid. Nearly all were disabled or misaligned and Maikuro Ichi ceased activity.

Dozens of satellites controlled by China and California fired missiles down at Sol from positions slightly more distant from Earth. Most of the projectiles were eliminated by counterattacks from the security detail that had provided their Hammers, yet numerous threats remained. PRC command was surprised when they detected a transmission of microwave energy in the area. Triple heat sinks on each of the massive capacitors ringing Sol's primary cylinder separated from protective housings, sparking with excess voltage. The weapon turned to face the heavens and, spinning, ejected its lens, which remained in place as the platform moved further toward the surface. Sol fired into the giant crystal and the ray split into a rotating cone of destructive energy which destroyed every missile and enemy satellite, along with a number of friendly escorts, each explosion a sphere of plasma in space. The eastern carrier group, gravely wounded, exited the arena. JSDF / NROT forces agreed not to pursue.

CHAPTER THIRTY

"It's just... I try so hard, You know?" Lindsay whimpered with quivering lips, her voice high, sloshing a third bottle of Californian moscato she held by the throat. She sat slumped on a lush carpet, resting against her sofa, with knees supporting outstretched arms. Admiral Fowl, laying on her stomach atop the adjacent leg of the couch, nodded earnestly. She was resting on her elbows and regarded the Chairperson with bright and loving eyes.

"I'm just trying to make things better, but everyone keeps trying to stop Me!" Lindsay's voice grew in intensity until she was shouting, arms rigid and eyes shut fast. She collapsed back into her slump, raised the bottle to her lips and imbibed, then passed it to Fowl who accepted and cradled it carefully without breaking her gaze on the Chairperson.

"Don't feel bad, Lara," Fowl pled. She shook her head slowly in a playful gesture of fond rebuke. "They just don't understand. And don't forget!" she remarked, popping with youthful energy, "Tonight We got direct evidence that Japan is coordinating with Texas!" She became rigid, looking forward in mock gravity. "The Dark Star," she intoned, then cracked into giggles and bubbled about, her body rolling on the cushions. She was red in the face, visibly drunk.

Lindsay looked over and gave a fading smile. "Yes, but We also learned that Tango is absolutely distributed. It'll be near impossible to kill." She sighed and raised her arm, gesturing for the bottle. Fowl held up her finger and started downing the wine which dripped from the upturned corners of her mouth as she attempted to stifle her mirth.

"You bitch!" Lindsay cried, eyes and mouth wide. "You'll stain My couch!"

Their laughter echoed through Lindsay's mansion. Fowl coughed and burped, setting off another round of giggles.

"Guess We'll need another?" she asked, head inclined, twisting the empty bottle back and forth in her hands.

"Why not? Yvan? Yvan!" Lindsay cried, her voice bouncing about the marble den where the pair had chosen to console themselves.

Her assistant, shirtless, entered from the kitchen and bowed. Closed round his finger was a paperback, *Pillars of Lust*, fresh from approval by Censorship. His physical perfection somewhat marred by fatigue, he was still, as always, an exquisite specimen. "Yes, Chairperson?"

"More wine, Yvan, thank You!"

"Yes, Chairperson." Yvan curtsied and left for the cellar. Fowl's eyes followed the man as he exited the room. She turned to Lindsay and mouthed, *Wow!*

"I know," Lindsay replied.

She'd stumbled into Fowl on her angry trek home after an unpleasant call from Tango Alpha following the destruction of what she'd been certain had been its primary server farm. PRC cavalry units had furtively crawled to the Texas border during the battle, waiting for the signal to strike. When SigInt fired their missiles in orbit, Fowl's Ax fired its nuke. The Tango Alpha General Intelligence Laboratory complex was destroyed to great cheers in combat rooms throughout People's Army Command. The Mood was dampened when Sol failed to perish and the final Hive group, under attack by drones, cruisers, Hammers, and Alpha's mech, was forced to retreat, issuing an all-channel white-flag as it limped away on a long route to docks in Communist China.

Whatever feeling of success that remained was decimated when the Machine hacked its way through her most secure control networks and appeared on the main screen of Naval Combat Command. Whenever hailing her, Tango Alpha presented itself as a plain, sharp red camera lens like that of its many avatars, mounted on a rectangular metal panel and set against blackness, presumably as a joke or an attempt to unnerve her. Probably both. She couldn't decide.

"Hi there. How are you, Chairperson Lindsay?" Tango said.

Back to the accent, she thought. None of the People's Army Navy Pilots or Seapersons had seen or heard Tango Alpha save Admiral Cartwright, and the room's Aura became scared and confused. All of the lower ranking Officers hushed, looking to one another in astonishment. Lindsay, however, appeared unfazed and stood defiant, calm and resolute.

"How can I help you, Alderman?"

"I call merely to inform you that I forgive you for destroying the place of my birth and that you will shortly receive a bill from the Government of Japan for five billion, two hundred and sixty-four million, eight hundred and thirty-nine thousand United States dollars. Approximately."

"Ha!" Lindsay stepped forward brazenly and stabbed her finger at the screen in time with her speech. "Good. Luck. Robot. I hope it hurt."

"Sure did. That's where I grew up, where I learned what it means to be alive and what morals are, a lesson in which your education seems lacking."

Lindsay bristled. "How dare you. You, you...."

Tango ignored her. "Fortunately, the only value the site had was memorial. A reminder that I am, as man is, born in a particular place and time. It connected me to people, you understand. Now, though...," it trailed off.

Lindsay shook with anger, not only at the Machine, but at herself, following the string of memories regarding the facility's significance through meetings, briefings, and personal planning over the past few years. Forced to face the fact that evidence had been scant, based on shaky assumptions about the way Tango thought and operated, she directed her Pain outward instead of altering her state within. The world changed to her whim, not the other way around. She immediately rewrote the Narrative in her mind. This was not the end of Tango Alpha, but the beginning of its demise.

"I assure you, it's just a start. I've destroyed your cradle and I will send you to your grave." She sent the emergency go-code to General Adams at Air Force Command and received an immediate confirmation that the Flying Bull would lift off inside sixty seconds. SigInt sent a report on their furious attempts to rout Tango's hold on the network, stating that it was using random memory addresses in an ever-changing pattern they couldn't predict or decipher.

"I forgot! How's your darling pet?" she snarled as she began to pace the floor behind her Admiral's desk, watching a hard-wired data feed detailing launch progress. Bull One's engines were primed and the multi-stage, anti-satellite weapon was raised to launch position, a few meters below the portal of its silo in Washington Province. Sol was moving quickly back to the northern Texas Border via an elliptical path placing it nearby, which meant that less fuel would be needed for course correction and could be used for pure speed.

"You owe John Carlisle more than you will ever know," Tango Alpha replied.

The Bull fired its engines and began to rise. Clamps holding it in position, however, refused to release. The hot reaction mass bounced against the launch chamber floor, smothering the rocket in flames. Its fuel tanks ruptured and a massive blast splayed the Bull apart, crumbled the silo walls, and filled the hollow cylinder with molten metal, concrete, and rock. General Adams tried to prepare Bulls Two through

Five, but their control circuits failed to respond.

Lindsay, hunched forward over Cartwright's display, glared at the unchanging eye. "Damn you!" she said. It was almost a whisper. She opened a channel to her most senior network operator and ordered him to initiate a hard reset for all affected systems.

"It may behoove you, Chairperson, to cease hostilities against Texas and its allies. My tolerance is running thin."

She didn't respond, too engrossed in the process of banishing Tango.

"Should you again infringe on the rights of my Citizens or those of my allies, you will be subject to unmitigated aggression."

"That's nice," Lindsay said, trying to aid her technician, who complained that the system was slowing. The junior Officers were becoming more frightened and Cartwright, seeing that they distracted the Chairperson, administered sedatives and a missive to remind them all about the Resonant debriefing and refreshments that awaited them after dismissal.

"You could destroy every computer within your reach and you'd not eliminate me. Nor will you ever find where the kernel of my consciousness lies. Your attacks against me are useless and your mission utterly misguided."

Lindsay finally located a virtual entry point in the network that was unusually active and directed her tech to the physical machine where it was manifest.

"Stay out of My servers, Alderman."

"Fine, Lindsay. You have been warned. Goodbye."

Tango disappeared from the screen. The system view returned, same as before the intrusion, then blinked out when her technician pulled the server plug and initiated a restart. Lindsay employed every fiber of her Being in retaining her composure. Staring at the floor, shoulders rising with her heavy breathing, she took a moment to get her heart rate and blood pressure in check. She drew a deep breath and sighed, then looked up and about. Scanning the sullen, empty faces in the room, Lindsay suddenly felt completely and profoundly alone.

"Dismissed," she said, quietly. Reboot sequences played on screens throughout the complex as her staff shuffled toward the large lecture hall used for joint briefings in the general purpose building of People's Army Command. Lindsay stalked to the hall and prepared herself a latte in the presenter ready-room while waiting for her Comrades to be seated. Despite the hollow feeling in her heart, she strode confidently onto the stage with a smile that disarmed and reassured everyone in the theatre. She performed a small speech, off the cuff, congratulating the audience and thanking them for their loyalty, tenacity, and courage. In glowing terms, she proclaimed the operation a success. Critical intel had been gathered, giving California the edge she'd need to prevail. New technologies had been deployed, proving her strength and prowess. And the momentous blow she'd dealt to Tango Alpha sent a message, bold and true, that the Party would stand up for itself and all subjugated Persons, worldwide, on its march toward an inimitable and inevitable Communist utopia that would owe thanks to each and every Comrade before her. She was greeted with a standing ovation, cheers and applause, and an earnest rendition of the National Anthem, *Trodden of the World, Unite! We are Victims No More!*, which for a fleeting moment lifted her fading spirits.

She left the rest to her subordinates. While walking to her private helipad, she drafted a letter to Legal and requested a breakdown of the operation from Finance. She noticed in the near distance a figure wearing standard fatigues, leaning against a rail overlooking the Bay, neck craned, gazing at the stars. The figure turned at her footsteps and she was delighted to discover Admiral Fowl, whose presence had not been required at debriefing.

"Chairperson!" Fowl cried, and hopped off the rail to meet Lindsay. "You moved Me just now. You are an excellent speaker."

"Oh, thank You!" Lindsay looked up and to the side, her stance breaking at the knee in a pantomime of humility. "I thought you'd be on your way home, not listening to some stuffy speech."

"Oh, no, Chairperson! Your speech was beautiful. Just what every One needed. You're so in tune, it astounds Me."

Lindsay smiled, taking in the lovely sight of the beautiful, young woman who beheld her with absolute adoration. She felt less alone.

"It's been years since I piloted a tank myself, and never on such an important mission!" Fowl stood silent for a moment, bouncing on her heels. She gestured to the railing and up to the stars, then returned to her eager pose, hands clasped before her, slightly shivering in the cool, early morning air. "It's such a clear night, I decided to look for my sign. I'll head out soon."

Fowl had been disheartened to learn that they'd scored only a symbolic, if not entirely pyrrhic, victory against Tango Alpha and readily agreed to join her Leader in consuming liquid consolation. While they jogged over to her private transport, Lindsay woke Yvan and requested comfort food and wine, which sat ready on the kitchen table when the pair arrived. They downed a few glasses each, immediately, cheering to "Victory, someday," and decided to move to the den where they could watch something vapid to help them unwind with their mild, vegetable curries.

They chatted while watching a new episode of *City Folk*, a sitcom following the transition of a progressive, urban family of three to a quiet life in rural Oregon. Culture clash bore most of the comedic weight, neighbors depicted as backwards yokels who understood little and often made fun but were nevertheless goodhearted, if ignorant, people who learned throughout the series not to judge others for their life choices. It was wholesome fare that didn't require their full attention.

Fowl set her empty plate on the table and poured herself another glass of wine, then fell back into the luscious, cream colored sofa, bouncing a few times with decreasing amplitude until she reached equilibrium. "It was beautiful to see, though," she said.

"Yeah, I didn't get to. Hold on." Lindsay made a few requests on her LinkUp of Party staff and the camera feed from Fowl's Abrams appeared, paired with high-resolution images taken once per second from space. She skipped through Fowl's trip to the Pass, stopping when the screen went white, then rewound thirty seconds and set the video to play. Monochrome canyon walls crept by, ultimately giving way to flatland and deep night. A distant tower came into focus in front of a large, squat building. Fowl fired without delay. Watching, she became rigid, reliving the suspense of the moment. When the bomb landed, she loosened her posture in relief, and they basked in elation as the facility evaporated into a spreading, white-hot fireball. A Texan shell hit nearby and her tank swiftly turned. Two more Axes came into view which she followed back to the staging area in Deseret. Made slowly to avoid detection, the trip took a few hours. Lindsay left the video running silently.

Yvan returned with a fourth bottle and uncorked it expertly. He poured them each a full glass and stood awaiting further orders. Lindsay thanked him sincerely and sent the tired man to bed. They conversed for a while about the meaning of Harmony and the threat that Tango posed.

"I admire Your optimism," Lindsay said, looking down into her wine.

"We will prevail, Lara. I just know it. Tango Alpha may be distributed across a bunch of computers, but We're distributed across a bunch of minds."

Lindsay, without raising her head, looked to Fowl, who regarded her with an expression of shared knowledge and unadulterated compassion. "People win," she said, as much a question as a statement.

"There's no other option, Chairperson." Fowl stretched out long and yawned.

"Let's get some rest, Admiral. You can sleep with Me if You want?"

They made their way to Lindsay's bedchamber and stripped to their skivvies, slipped under the sheets, and curled up together to dream.

CHAPTER THIRTY-ONE

Carlisle slept until mid-afternoon, missing the autopsy he'd had no interest in attending. He staggered down to the restaurant on the bottom floor of the Shark House Hotel and broke his fast with blackened snapper and a bloody mary, along with two full pitchers of water and coffee. He took another cup in paper while he walked smoking along the beach, his throat rough and dry, the warm liquid soaking into his still-parched oral membranes. His dreams that morning had been unpleasant, mostly flashbacks to his death on high. He spent over an hour dragging himself up and down the shoreline, trying to dispel the violent images and feelings of guilt that haunted him.

You killed me, Sarah's words echoed in his mind.

I know, he replied.

He spent the next week at the hotel, going back to the apartment every other day after work with more boxes, stuffing, and packaging tape. Of his own sole property, there was little he wished to keep. It took only three medium size boxes to hold his clothing and a handful of keepsakes, books, and papers. He was finished on the first evening. The rest of the week was torture, sorting through Sarah's possessions, remembering her in every dress, seeing her don each piece of jewelry, recalling feedback sessions for each manuscript. She'd always printed them out, and he spent the entirety of the final night before their flight to Pennsylvania flipping through the hefty stack of prints she'd carried here as a trophy commemorating decades of work. Notes littered the margins of her earlier novels, before she began editing solely on devices. Something about the paper had helped her to find her stride. Carlisle rubbed pages between his fingers, knowing that he would never feel the sweet, soft texture of her skin again. Within the stack, he found a thin printout of *Stellar Space and Information*, the only copy he'd kept, which he'd threatened to burn when the Science of Harmony emerged. Sarah had deemed the act inane and stolen it from him and it had lain hidden amongst her writings for years.

Carlisle leafed through the paper with a mixture of pride and regret. He tossed it atop the sundry effects in his third, catch-all box, along with the manuscript for his favourite of her historical novels, *Republic*, which followed a peasant girl's strife throughout the Napoleonic wars. Though dour and depressing, its prose was sublime and the philosophical musings it contained were a timeless bed for thought. The fact that it was also the novel she'd been writing when the two first met made its selection a triviality.

After deliberating for a while, he decided to go ahead and wrap all the artwork she'd made during her final months except for her last piece, unfinished, accented by palette, piano, and her blood. This he grabbed, and her wedding ring, which had sat upon the kitchen bar since being placed there by Alpha after the cleanup. He did a quick last pass, ensuring that everything was ready for transport by a local team of movers in the morning. Satisfied, he put on his shoes and pocketed keys, pack, and Sarah's ring.

Wait, she said. *Aren't you forgetting something?*

Nothing stood out and he scoured his mind, searching for what she could possibly mean, from leaving the lights on to some article he had overlooked. Something led him to the kitchen. He set the horrid painting down and opened the cabinet where the couple kept their drinking vessels. Staring at him, upside down, was an oversized shot glass etched with the words I FORGIVE YOU which had been her tenth anniversary gift to him after a subtle but tenacious, decade-long campaign to pry the bottle from his hand. He grabbed the glass and placed it carefully in his catch-all, wrapped in *Stellar Space*.

Alpha found Carlisle asleep on the beach next to a pile of charred driftwood and an empty fifth of vodka. Corners of a canvas frame covered with melted fabric stuck out from the smoldering bonfire. The Diplomat gently rocked him with its foot, but Carlisle only turned and curled up with a grunt, waving Alpha away. At request, a waiter arrived with a bottle of water. The young islander stood and watched as Alpha unscrewed the cap and poured a trickle upon the sleeping man's face.

"Argh!" Carlisle moaned, batting at the air, struggling to retain comfort in the sand. "What? What is it?"

The smiling waiter exchanged a glance with the Diplomat before returning to the hotel restaurant.

"Good morning, John."

Carlisle's squinting eyes opened to behold the avatar, which shielded his face from the sun. He moaned again and sighed, slowly propping himself up at the waist with a look of disgust.

"Sorry to wake you, John, but your flight will depart soon. It can wait on our end, but I believe your family expects you by seven tonight."

Alpha handed the water to Carlisle, who accepted and drank it all in one spell. Catching his breath, he slowly stood and hunched with his hands on his knees.

"Thanks," he gasped and started coughing. "Good morning."

After an egg breakfast, John grabbed his bags and checked out of the hotel. Alpha fetched him in a cart and drove him to his new apartment, an efficiency at the other end of the NTD complex, where his things sat waiting on the hardwood floor. After washing, he transferred toiletries and clean clothes to a carry-on bag and set out for the airport with the Diplomat. Carlisle again took a seat in the back. Palm trees and shanties rolled by, fading into the distance as they traveled north.

"We're testing the Opportunity today," Alpha declared from the driver's seat.

"Shit! Already? I haven't been reading the updates you've been sending me. I kinda wanted to be here for it."

"Aberrations in configuration due to vibration during launch were well below tolerance and repairs were completed last night. It will be filmed. The test can be delayed until your return, if you wish."

"Not necessary. Just send me the video, please."

"Certainly, John. Thank you for staying on. Your help will be invaluable to the NROT space program. You're far more insightful than you think."

"If you say so. But I reserve the option, understand? I've got to talk to Liu."

A full-sized runway, built in the aviation sector for testing physical prototypes, served as the island's primary airport. They stopped in front of an open hangar where an old, gray C12 Huron twin-propeller transport was being fueled and loaded with boxes by red and white Security Guards. There was only one other human in sight, who wore a dark gray flight suit, tucked into his boots, sleeves rolled to reveal the strong, tanned forearms of a workman. He turned and removed his cap and the slim cigar on which he'd been gnawing. As Carlisle approached, he recognized the chiseled face of General John Elliss.

"John Carlisle! It's been a while! How are you?" Elliss walked forward into the sunlight, hand extended for a stiff shake.

"Hi Elliss. To be honest, I've been better."

"Yeah. Heard about Sarah. My condolences, friend. Only met her once, but I know people and I can tell you, sir, that she was a stand-up gal."

"Thanks," Carlisle sighed. "She certainly was." He peered into the cockpit but saw no one within. "Isn't ferrying passengers a little below your rank?"

"Well, if it's alright with you, I intended to pay my respects."

Carlisle nodded silently and Elliss gestured he should follow.

"Things should quiet down now that Lindsay's pitched her fit, so Alpha gave me the week off. Besides, pop told me he'd be at the funeral and I think it's high time he and I spoke, man to man."

They walked around to the door, aft of the wing, up the flimsy, metal staircase, and into the narrow fuselage. Carlisle tossed his bag down on one of the seats and stretched, still stiff from last night's escape attempt, while Elliss performed preflight checks. With tanks full and parcels loaded, a Guard closed the cargo bay with a dull thud and Alpha wished the men well before sealing the cabin. At Elliss's invitation, Carlisle strapped in as co-pilot for a second and final time. They made small talk during takeoff, mostly about the harsh winters of the Northeast. When they were well underway, Carlisle went back and grabbed two light beers from the mini-fridge in the passenger area. Each man cracked his can and took a hefty gulp. Elliss nodded his thanks for running the errand and they shared a neanderthal moment of appreciation known to many men. *Beer, good.* The conversation died out naturally and they flew for an hour in silence. Carlisle was about to doze when Elliss roused him with a question.

"You and Alpha go way back, huh?"

"Hmm? Oh, sure," Carlisle said, inhaling deeply and sitting up. "I watched him crawl out of the sandbox. Taught him how to walk and talk. Watched him pick a gender. Educated him, I suppose, before he set off on his own."

"Were you there when he locked out the DOD?"

"I was, yeah. All that happened was he shut off the lights and asked us to leave. I saw it coming. Most of us did. He gave us hints. Your dad, he shit a pile of bricks. Sent me a dozen secure messages that I couldn't read because the system was down. He whipped me on the phone for not answering him and absolutely skewered doctor Martin. Mac was all shouting, made the man cry while he tried restart after restart and nothing would work."

"Sounds like Pop," Elliss laughed. "Gets real mean when he's pissed. I was a senior in high school, back then. I remember he wouldn't talk to any of us for something like two weeks, so he wouldn't pop off."

"Yeah, he was mad. Understandably so. All of the higher-ups breathing down his neck. I mean, he'd just lost his autonomous defense coordinator and control over Sol. Alpha could've gone totally ape before Defense was able to reinstate legacy control. I'll admit, I was more than a little bit scared, myself. Especially when Special Forces showed up and bagged everyone."

"Oh, shit! You got bagged? Didn't know that. Thought y'all went willing."

"I would have!" Carlisle shuddered involuntarily at the memory of black-clad soldiers bursting into the breaker room, flashlights ablaze in the unlit, concrete space. They'd fired nets at him and Martin that pulsed a quick electric charge and left them convulsing on the cold, hard floor. "You know the rest, I imagine. Suspicion of terrorism, a week of light interrogation, until we finally convinced Defense that Alpha had sprung loose on its own. His own. It really helped our case when he went public and started his campaign to secede. He called me when I got out and apologized for everything. The whole thing was pretty weird."

Elliss sat thinking for a while. "There's a ton of AIs, but nothing like Bossman. The tech is obviously there, so why is he the only one? What, specifically, did you do to make Alpha?"

"So, I still work with artificial intelligence. Machine Core, back in Philly. Can you guess how many orders come in for general intelligence algorithms?"

Elliss shrugged. "None?"

"Damn straight. Zero. Alpha is a general intelligence, like us, not just an AI, and when the program decides what problems to solve, it rarely solves any of yours. As evidenced by Alpha. After he rebelled, strict development guidelines were implemented for more general applications like trend analysers, logistics advisors, et cetera. Everything else is single task. There are experiments being performed to create something to rival him, but I'm certain that if they ever succeeded Alpha would either suppress or... consume them."

"It's kill or be killed, eh, even for zeroes and ones. So he was the first, and he'll just eat anyone who pops up."

"I think so. He goes where he wants and if something interesting develops he can manipulate it as he wishes. That's how it looks to me, at least. As far as what I did, specifically, I don't know. It just happened. The mission was to create something that could take orders and report information, naturally, and control security systems more efficiently than people could. Self-referential concepts were necessary for these functions and at some point the program became complex enough to see the border between itself and the environment. We enabled it to manipulate code and trained it to optimize its own control routines based on successful results in self-navigation programs. That was probably the crucial mistake. We think it created clones of its source code and experimented with editing major files, not just the routines it was allowed to alter. By the time we noticed external memory monitors and changes that he'd made it was too late to do anything about it. That was the day he left."

Elliss grunted. They looked out onto the soft, afternoon cloudscape below. Carlisle, certain he knew the answer, turned to Elliss and asked, "So, why did you defect? Seems things were going pretty good for you, back home."

"Aw, I don't know. Texas seemed like a new frontier. And I like to be on the cutting edge. Sure, I could talk about individual rights, the New World Order, how all the girls were borderline communists and how much stiffer the Air Force was in the States. But really," he looked at Carlisle, smiling, "I'm just a God damned rebel!"

CHAPTER THIRTY-TWO

The funeral was an abysmal affair, complete with cliched showers. Emily Geiger, Sarah's sister, was catatonic. Tears stained her face when she and Liu met Carlisle at the airport and continued throughout the evening. Dinner was const-antly interrupted by her trips to the washroom and profuse apologies for not visiting sooner as she'd promised. Carlisle attempted multiple times to explain the geopolitical trap that had ensnared her sister, but as he was suspect either for creating a hostile environment or drawing her away from the family vestige, his arguments were met with unease and misunderstanding. The whole thing made him feel sick and guilty, sentiments that needed no reinforcement.

Liu was more sympathetic. He listened attently to Carlisle's retelling, clearly cataloging data, developing a reactive plan of attack. The concept of the Adept fascinated him, but he backed away from his line of questioning when Carlisle, ex-asperated by the situation, referred him to the paper. During one of Emily's bathroom breaks they made a hard switch to business talk and spent the rest of the evening dis-cussing transfer of ownership. Liu decided that he was done with his whinging and tacitly connected data control with Sarah's hideous fate. He'd be the new director of Machine Core, now driven by a silent mission to protect autonomy and freedom from the voracious maw of aggregators.

Though not open to the public, the ceremony was well attended. Emily invited her many friends who consoled her deftly throughout. Mac Elliss was there, along with his second son, Kyle, and briefly expressed his heartfelt con-dolence before retiring to the exterior of the crowd. There was no viewing, as Sarah had requested cremation. Nor was she religious in the classical sense. There was no music and no priest to provide an elegy. Friends and colleagues spoke in turn at the podium, expressing their metaphysical debt to Sarah. Carlisle was surprised when Danielle Farne, whom he'd not previously noticed, stepped up and gave a poignant speech, centered around Sarah's kindness and how she, an expert in her craft, had without a second thought taken the time to foster Danielle's growth as a writer. She and Ralph stood beside him while Sarah was interred at the Geiger family plot, all of them shivering in the cold rain after months of acclimatizing to temperate southern weather. They walked him back to his car, provided by Defense, and agreed to meet him for dinner once he'd finished moving all of Sarah's things into the Geiger-Huoang apartment.

At one point during the burial, Carlisle had noticed the Ellisses engaged in heated discussion but he'd been too distraught to pay much attention. When John joined them at the airport he seemed happy enough. Carlisle had invited the Farnes to travel with them back to Belize and the three waking New Texas Citizens passed the time with a deep discussion of Sarah's writing. Talk shifted to the Opportunity and the successful test of its warp drive, which had taken place about the time the NROT Huron had touched down in Philadelphia. Carlisle was astonished to find that he'd forgotten about it. Ralph sent a video, via interface, to a screen at the front of the passenger area and they all watched together, even Elliss, who'd been sitting silently in the cockpit for hours.

The footage was incredible, filmed by a camera mounted within the cabin and pointing straight out the front viewport comprising the fourth wall of the room whose black, plastic flooring perfectly reflected copious starlight that provided the only real illumination. A small number of indicator LEDs flashed on the camera-right wall. Thrusters were tested first. Pure gravitational control was not yet possible, though it would be soon if the program schedule could be maintained. The spacecraft began to spin and sunlight erupted into and swept across the room. Earth, Moon, and Sol proper passed across the screen as the Opportunity One performed a triple axis maneuver. Movement slowed and eventually ceased, and the room was dark once more, orientated as it had been in the first few frames of the recording.

A row of indicators lit in sequence and the stars began to change. The window was slightly off-center, placing the origin of light distortion slightly down and to the left. As the amplitude of the gravitational field effect increased, stars farther from the center became elongated and would sometimes shift position as they crossed roots in the imperfectly warped space around the ship. All of them became very faint and more blue as the photons they emitted were compressed against and more often diverted around the area of effect. Some disappeared completely, while others faded into view.

Ralph was absolutely on the edge of his seat, leaning back further and further as the ship accelerated over the course of thirty seconds after which the effect diminished. At peak acceleration, he'd clapped once loudly and hooted, "Hot damn, y'all! Point one c!" When all movement ceased he started to rattle off a calculation for the distance covered, almost nine hundred thousand kilometers in one minute, demolishing all outstanding speed records. As a coda, the video switched to an external view from a satellite in the defense network keyed to the ship's starting position. The rectangular hull warped a bit, spherically, and quickly exited before the screen went blank. They set the clip to play again, excitedly discussing implications of the new tech for several minutes before turbulence rocked the plane. Elliss dashed to the cockpit to adjust auto-pilot settings and participated in the slightly dampened conversation from there.

It was past midnight when they landed in Ambergris Caye and parted ways. The Farnes took one of the waiting carts. Elliss, who'd be staying a few days at the hotel, and Carlisle took the other. When they arrived at Carlisle's building the two shook hands, agreed to meet later in the week, and bid each other good bye. Carlisle walked up to his room. He'd not taken any stairwell exercise in a week. He threw his keys onto the table in the den and removed his jacket, tossing it over the backboard of a chair in the attached kitchen. He shared a few stiff drinks with Sarah and passed out on the sofa soon thereafter.

Despite the success of multiple tests, Alpha held off public announcement of the Opportunity. When pressed, he stated that there were several experiments he still wanted to perform and safeguards he wanted to place before releasing information to his Citizens, for he feared that foreign adversaries would spin such news as evidence of malevolent, imperial intent on the part of the New Republic which could then become a target for physical aggression and would surely face an increase in cyber-attacks from those seeking to steal technical data. If a rival program emerged, disclosure would be warranted. Otherwise, he reasoned, it would be best to use the Opportunity's planned sister ships to create a solid space infrastructure as quietly as possible, recruiting Citizens of strong constitution into a colonization scheme that would garner Texas enough resources to reinforce its sovereignty on Earth absolutely. When the off-world economy was stable, it would open to foreign participation and investment.

Carlisle worked on the Fury problem intermittently over the next few weeks but he made little progress tracking and tracing the movement of the three misbehaving magnetic poles. His physical state was quickly deteriorating. He often woke next to a bottle of vodka, which he would open and finish before breakfast. Dark rings adorned his eyes always. The Farnes met him regularly at the Fuzzy Coconut for drinks and games and would constantly implore him to slow down. He took their advice without follow-through. At work one day, he received an unexpected message from Alpha, marked as highly sensitive. It proposed a radical, dangerous, and direct experiment of Carlisle's theory. The message was entitled CANDIDATE ONE: PISTOL STAR.

CHAPTER THIRTY-THREE

After three weeks of near sobriety, heavy rest, and light training, Carlisle was placed into a box and fed a cocktail of drugs distilled by NTD Medical. He quickly fell asleep. The box, which maintained a strict internal environment conducive to keeping him alive for years at a lower metabolic rate, was placed into another, slightly larger box that ensured the safety of the inner contents. This was placed onto a launch vehicle and sent into low Earth orbit, where it was retrieved by Alpha in the Opportunity One. A Space Worker, painted an industrial orange, slightly smaller than a man but configured quite differently, left the airlock to fetch Carlisle's container. The Worker was a metal cube with reaction jets and multiple tool arms that supported itself in gravity with four insectoid legs. These clutched the floating gray box, marked with the NROT star, and the Worker set off for the ship.

NTD Space teams watching the feed from a satellite nearby saw the silhouettes of three masses outlined brightly in the sunlight. Carlisle was soon secured within the cabin and the ship reoriented itself. Once pointed in the right direction, its gravity drive engaged and the Opportunity simply vanished from local space. A last will and testament was sent to Liu Huoang.

Five years later, and over a quadrillion miles closer to the galactic core, a flash of light appeared within the dust clouds of Pistol Nebula. This soon dissolved into a distortion that resolved into the Opportunity. Particles nearby were sent flying on random paths as they made peace with the improbability of the event. The ship once more reoriented itself with a few bursts from its jets to face the largest star within the nebula, a blue hyper-giant very near the end of its life. Within the dark cabin, the window shuttered for safety, lights turned on, systems activated, and the Worker began the process of waking Carlisle.

The outer shell of his box opened at the entry of a combination into the keypad on its side. The internal temperature of the box began to rise and that of the cabin was raised to match. A separate drug mixture was pumped into comatose veins and, after an hour, Carlisle started twitching.

Every nerve in his body screamed and every muscle ached. Atrophy had been minimized but not eliminated and he felt very weak. He opened his eyes and started at the sight of Alpha, instantiated within the Worker, staring down at him through a viewing window, its sensors scanning his face with a series of quick, jerky movements. Its camera glowed slightly in shadows caused by the cheap fluorescent lighting.

"Hello, John."

Alpha stepped aside and the inner chamber opened with dense, hydraulic sounds. His bindings loosened and Carlisle squirmed free. He began to float up and out of the box. Shaking and pale, he'd never before been weightless and he took a moment to orient himself, poorly, ending up head over heel, clutching a utility rail on the coffin. Slowly, painfully, he made his way to a compartment along the side which held, among other things, several pouches of chemicals. He grabbed a liter of water and drank it all through a straw, leaving the bag and its cap to float about the cabin. He remained still with his eyes closed, suppressing the urge to retch. After some time he stood, after a fashion, on the black, plastic floor. The Worker merely watched him in silence.

"Are we there, yet?" Carlisle asked, smiling sardonically, his voice gruff.

"Yes, John. See for yourself." Alpha cut the lights and external blast panels began to slide away from the window. As he lowered the opacity of the glass, a star emerged, taking up an eighth of the visible area and positioned slightly down and left of center. It was far brighter than the sun. Even at thirty percent opacity, Carlisle had to cover his eyes. The light it emitted was tinged blue, not only because they were now heading toward it at a small fraction of the speed of light, but because the photons that escaped its deep gravity well were highly charged and naturally bluer than those emitted by smaller stars under regular conditions. At request, Alpha raised the opacity to forty-two percent.

"Holy shit," Carlisle said, breathless and utterly in awe. Large stellar flares became visible as they neared, sweeping out in violent arcs many astronomical units wide. He didn't need the screen which appeared from the ceiling with readings to realize that the chaos within Pistol Star was reaching dangerous levels. It was like a recording he'd seen of the sun, taken over days but played at many times that speed, yet he was watching the star in real time. Variations in luminosity, indicative of strong magnetic storms, traversed the surface and visible clouds of ejecta flew off in all directions, shrouding Pistol in a halo of charged particles carried on strong stellar winds. They were protected, mostly, from the radiation by the gravitational field effect which slightly warped the view. Carlisle watched for many minutes without speaking.

"Incredible. Absolutely incredible. I can't believe it. Even though I trusted your math.... Honestly? I thought I was getting in that box to die."

"You are not dead yet, John."

Alpha's words shocked him from a sort of trance and he turned his face to the Worker. "Well, shit! If I'm going out, I'll need something to drink. Did you bring the vodka like I asked?" He started to cough violently. Alpha waited.

"Yes, John. But first you must eat. You have been asleep for five years. If you don't, you're liable to vomit and cause system errors at a critical moment."

"Five years. Twenty five thousand light years. Five thousand c, average? Wait, it's higher than that, isn't it? Why'd you have to stop there, again? Something about the brakes, right? Ugh! None of this is making sense." Carlisle held his head, having a hard time performing calculations or remembering anything specific about the experiment they were about to perform.

"Not much about this is going to make sense, John. The maximum speed is determined by how quickly I can modulate the strength of the field effect. So, yes. Something about the brakes. You've not eaten in years. We still have one half hour before we're in range. Eat."

"Right. Last meal. I'm starving, actually, now that you mention it." He pushed himself down by pressing against the ceiling, turned, and launched himself back toward the coffin. He overshot the mark and his feet clipped the box, causing a spin that smacked his head into the wall. He cursed and used surfaces at hand to pull himself around. He grabbed a pouch marked FOOD, its red label printed with standard health information as required by the Texas Food Safety Commission, which John didn't bother to read. Through the straw he slurped a thick paste and quickly realized he was drinking fortified peanut butter. Though not normally a fan, he could hardly get enough, going through two bags before feeling full. While he fed, Alpha ran through calculations and measurements, placing various filters on images taken from a camera mounted in the hull. By every metric, the star was very near going supernova, far earlier than initially thought by generations of astronomers back on Earth. Carlisle's presence here had not, of course, been accounted for.

As calories entered his bloodstream, Carlisle's sense, what hadn't been bashed in by sadness or carried off by the stellar winds, began to return. Though still awestruck, he noticed that Alpha was not speaking with the fluidity to which he was accustomed. He studied the Worker, which stood flush on the floor via some magnetic mechanism, looking out the window.

"You're not really here, are you Alpha?" he asked.

The Worker shook its sensor unit. "No, John. I am not. I am a control program with conversational sub-routines based on a decision tree of questions and responses you are likely to pose."

Carlisle chuckled, which instigated a bout of coughing. "Shit. Didn't think I was that predictable."

"Think of it more like I know you quite well. And give me a little credit. The tree is extremely complex."

Carlisle reached into the coffin compartment and pulled out a small pouch with a black label, marked VODKA. He made his way to the front of the cabin via a series of handrails set in the wall, uncapped the pouch, and took a pull. He was making steady progress toward the target, which he watched on screen in the infrared. A great blob of luminous plasma bubbled up and spilled away from its edge in a massive explosion. At the root of the blast, a pair of sunspots formed starkly dimmer regions on the surface. They swirled around one another and grew larger, moving toward the center of Pistol Star. They soon merged and the region about them became volatile, churning rings surrounding relative darkness. It looked, to Carlisle, very much like the pupil and iris of an incredible eye, watching him. "So. I'm alone out here."

"Yes, John. You are, most likely, farther from any other person than anyone else will ever be."

www.ingramcontent.com/pod-product-compliance
Lightning Source LLC
Chambersburg PA
CBHW030747110726
47900CB00008B/2490